OCEANS of PLASTIC

UNDERSTANDING AND SOLVING A POLLUTION PROBLEM

TRACEY GRAY

© Tracey Gray 2022
First printed 2022. This reprint 2023.

All rights reserved. Except under the conditions described in the *Australian Copyright Act 1968* and subsequent amendments, no part of this publication may be reproduced, stored in a retrieval system or transmitted in any form or by any means, electronic, mechanical, photocopying, recording, duplicating or otherwise, without the prior permission of the copyright owner. Contact CSIRO Publishing for all permission requests.

Tracey Gray asserts their right to be known as the author of this work.

A catalogue record for this book is available from the National Library of Australia.

ISBN: 9781486312573 (pbk)
ISBN: 9781486312580 (epdf)
ISBN: 9781486316847 (epub)

Published by:
CSIRO Publishing
36 Gardiner Road, Clayton VIC 3168
Private Bag 10, Clayton South VIC 3169
Australia

Telephone: +61 3 9545 8400
Email: publishing.sales@csiro.au
Website: www.publish.csiro.au
Sign up to our email alerts: publish.csiro.au/earlyalert

Edited by Nan McNab
Cover, text design and layout by Cath Pirret Design
Cover photo by Rich Carey; cover illustrations by Good Studio
Illustrations on pp. 8, 11–13, 16, 18, 22–23, 25, 27, 29, 34, 38–39, 44–45, 47, 50, 53–54, 57, 59–60, 62, 68–69, 74, 96, 100 and 102 by Envisage Information Technology based on concepts by Tracey Gray
Other illustrations by Good Studio (pp. 1, 2, 4, 5, 14, 15 and repeated throughout); Maquiladora (dolphins throughout; whale on p. 28); Andrew Rybalko (p. 30); Roi and Roi (bottle on p. 38); ekler (p. 93)
Printed by Ingram Lightning Source

The views expressed in this publication are those of the author and illustrator and do not necessarily represent those of, and should not be attributed to, the publisher or CSIRO.

CSIRO acknowledges the Traditional Owners of the lands that we live and work on and pays its respect to Elders past and present. CSIRO recognises that Aboriginal and Torres Strait Islander peoples in Australia and other Indigenous peoples around the world have made and will continue to make extraordinary contributions to all aspects of life including culture, economy and science. CSIRO is committed to reconciliation and demonstrating respect for Indigenous knowledge and science. The use of Western science in this publication should not be interpreted as diminishing the knowledge of plants, animals and environment from Indigenous ecological knowledge systems.

Note for readers: Words in bold are explained in the glossary at the end of the book.

Note for teachers: Teacher notes are available at:
https://www.publish.csiro.au/book/7926/#forteachers

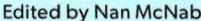

Oct25_RP_ILS

CONTENTS

Introduction   4

Chapter 1.   The role of our oceans   7
Chapter 2.   Slow-motion oceans   20
Chapter 3.   Catching a current   31
Chapter 4.   Great oceans! It's a garbage patch!   37
Chapter 5.   A lifetime of plastic   48
Chapter 6.   Impacts on oceanic wildlife   56
Chapter 7.   Marine science in action   70
Chapter 8.   Communities for change   79
Chapter 9.   Ideas, inspirations and innovators   91
Chapter 10.   Action for the oceans   99

Further information   113
Glossary   114
Index   119

INTRODUCTION

We use plastic every day, from the moment we wake up to when we switch off our lights at night. Our day is packed with plastic. It is woven into our clothes and wrapped around our food. We play on plastic and we even tie our shoelaces with plastic. There is no question that plastic is a part of our lives. Plastic may be fantastic, but it is affecting our planet. Tiny pieces of plastic are now found in the air, water and oceans.

How many stars can you see on a clear night in the sky? It's hard to count them all, with over 1 trillion stars out there! Scientists estimate that there are more pieces of plastic in the ocean than visible stars in the Milky Way. If we do nothing, by 2050 there will be more pieces of plastic by weight, than fish, in the ocean!

Get ready because we are going on an ocean-sized adventure! We're going to discover the importance of our oceans to all living things and dive into the world of ocean plastics. We'll explore ocean gyres and investigate how plastic pieces break up into smaller and smaller pieces. We'll find out why marine creatures are mistakenly eating plastic, and how plastic is making its way along the marine food chain – right onto your dinner plate!

Along the way we'll learn from scientists, be inspired by ocean activists and see how community programs help to prevent ocean plastics. We can do so much to help. Our everyday actions can create powerful positive change. We can use knowledge, ideas and inspiration to make the changes we need to stop the flow of plastic. Together we can become ocean change-makers!

How to use this book

The words in **bold** are explained in the Glossary. These terms and concepts will help you increase your knowledge about oceans, **plastics** and marine **ecosystems**.

You might see a name in italics and in brackets after the common name of a creature; for example, green sea turtle (*Chelonia mydas*). This is the unique scientific name for that **species**.

Fact boxes and creature features contain fun facts and amazing information helping you to explore ocean plastics.

Lastly, there are things you can do to help: practical ways to reduce plastic in your daily life and information about inspirational groups and organisations that you can join, as well as new ideas and solutions to inspire you as ocean change-makers.

Chapter 1

THE ROLE OF OUR OCEANS

Our watery world

Over 70 per cent of the Earth is covered in water. Oceans are huge. They hold around 97 per cent of Earth's water. Oceans create weather, make clouds, bring rain, push wind and power storms. All land plants and animals rely on water from the weather created by oceans to survive.

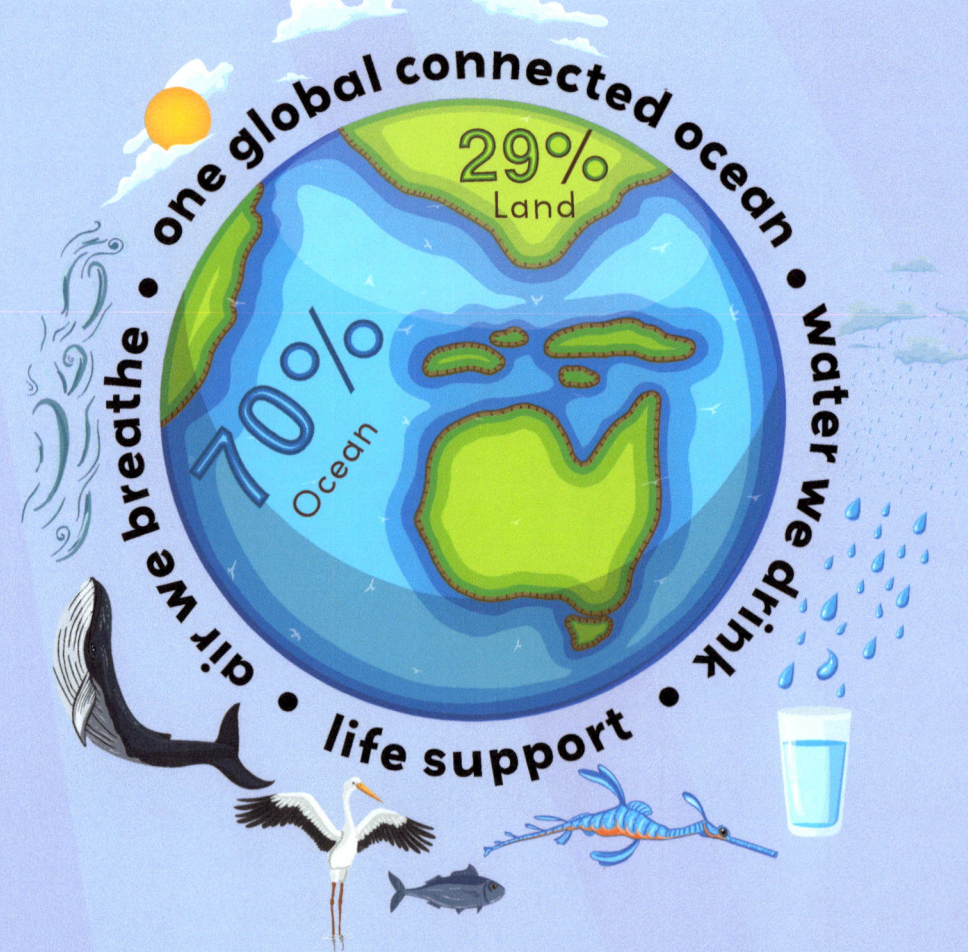

Planet Earth is home to one global ocean covering 70 per cent of the planet. The ocean is connected to every living thing on the planet. Oceans create the air we breathe, water we drink and food we eat. We depend on oceans.

Chapter 1: The role of our oceans

Oceans create the fresh air we breathe, the water we drink, water for farms and provides us with food we eat. Oceans help control Earth's temperature. Ocean waters can store large amounts of heat as warm water. The water moves around in ocean **currents**, helping to keep the Earth's temperature stable and warm. Oceans assist the climate, by taking in **carbon dioxide** and keeping it out of the **atmosphere**. Oceans create **oxygen** – about 70 per cent of the world's oxygen is produced in oceans!

Most importantly of all, oceans are home to our planet's incredible marine life, from tiny **krill** to massive blue whales. Deep-sea vampire squids, icy narwhals, leafy sea dragons, sharks, flying fish, and spinner dolphins are just some of the fantastic creatures that live in marine **habitats**. Our frozen oceans, cool temperate seas, marine trenches and **tropical** reefs all support ecosystems containing an amazing variety of living things.

Without oceans, there would be no life on Earth. Every living thing on Earth is connected to the ocean in some way. Let's dive in to find out how they power our world.

The ocean is home

Oceans are the largest living spaces we have on the Earth! Oceans take up more space on the Earth's surface than land. To fill our oceans, we would need a massive 1.35 billion cubic kilometres of saltwater! Now that's a lot of water. The salty water is held in one large, interconnected ocean, which is divided into five great oceans. These are, in order of size from largest to smallest: the Pacific, Atlantic, Indian, Southern and Arctic oceans. The **equator** runs through the Pacific, Atlantic and Indian oceans, and each has warm tropical waters and cold temperate seas. The Arctic Ocean surrounds the North Pole and at the South Pole, Antarctica, is surrounded by the Southern Ocean. The Arctic and Southern oceans are the coldest oceans because they are super cooled by the Earth's polar ice caps.

Seas are smaller parts of an ocean and are often surrounded by land. Think of the Mediterranean Sea, the Black Sea, the Red Sea, the Caribbean Sea or the Arafura Sea. Seas are usually smaller and shallower than oceans.

The sun-filled upper layers of oceans and seas are home to over 90 per cent of marine life. In the shallow edges of the oceans and seas live soft seaweed, beautiful corals, seagrass meadows, mangroves and mudflats, which provide homes for all types of **organisms**. Further down in some parts of the ocean giant kelp forests and bright sponge gardens grow.

Out in the open oceans, swarms of small **zooplankton** called krill are the favourite food of the most gigantic creatures that have ever lived on Earth – enormous blue whales.

Deep underwater, where sunlight cannot reach and pressure is extreme, mysterious creatures use light to attract prey. Each is adapted to survive in some of the most extreme conditions on the planet.

Marine habitats

Marine habitats are important underwater places where different species are found based on their environmental needs. These needs may include the temperature of the water, the amount of light, the **salinity** (saltiness) of the water, the amount of **nutrients** (food) or the type of shelter. Marine habitats include seagrass beds, kelp forests, rockpools, rocky shores, tropical reefs, mangroves, mudflats, coral reefs and sea ice floes.

Marine ecosystems

Ecosystems are exciting places where living things compete, work together and share resources. A marine ecosystem contains different living and non-living things. Imagine a kelp forest, with long brown kelp fronds reaching to the surface. Fish, sea snails, sea stars and seals live here, they are all connected to each other. They eat, hunt, share homes, find mates or rear their young in their ecosystem. All of these interactions make the ecosystem work.

▶

Mighty marine ecosystems are home to many different organisms, living together and creating marine habitats. The ocean is alive with things that depend on each other to survive.

Chapter 1: The role of our oceans

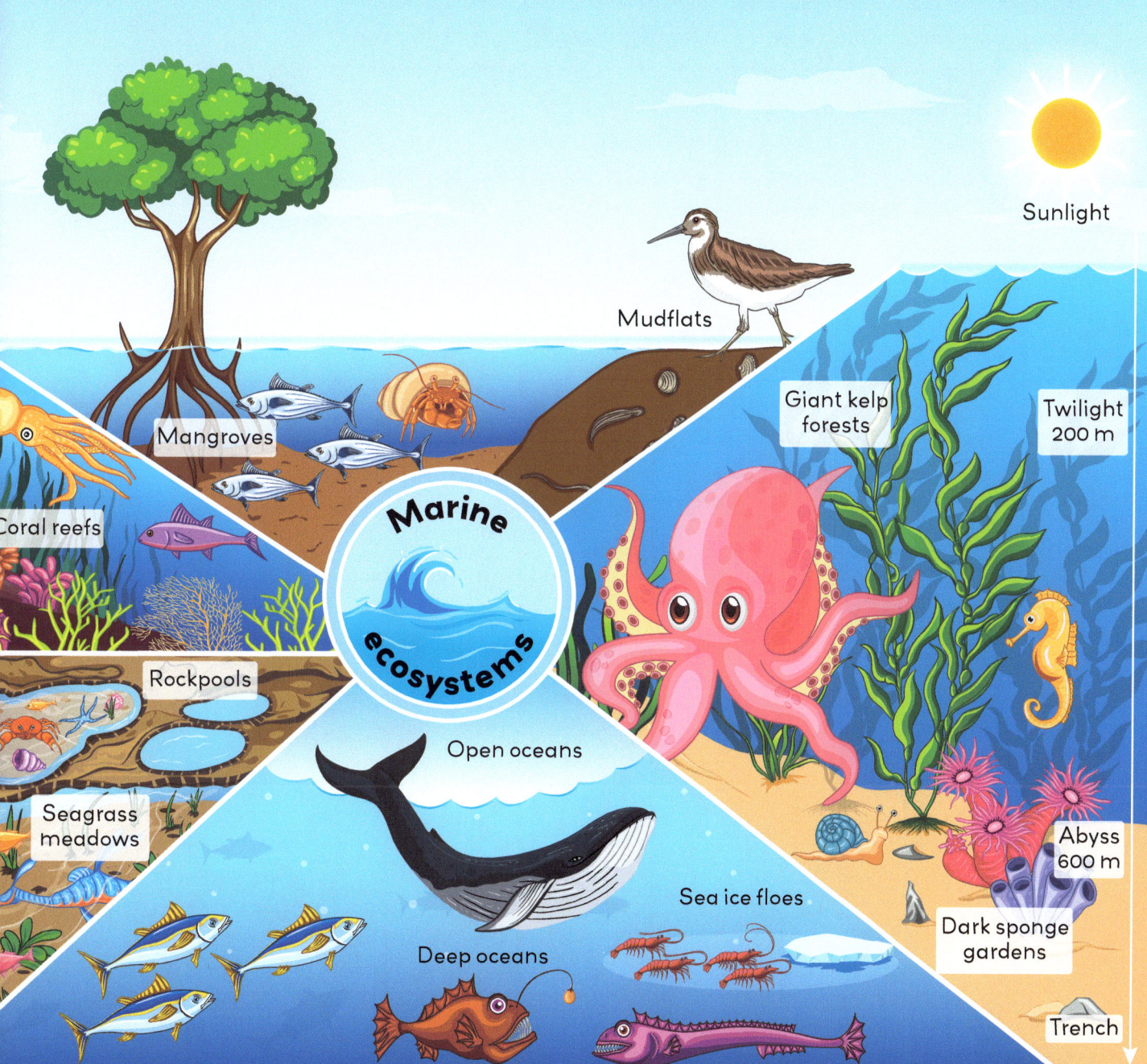

Oceans and water cycle

Every drop of water has been on the Earth for millions of years! Moving around in a constant **water cycle**. The world's oceans fuel the water cycle. When energy from the sun heats water, it **evaporates**, changing from a liquid into an invisible gas – water **vapour**. Water vapour is warm and light, so it rises up into the atmosphere. As it rises, the water vapour cools down. The water **molecules** join together creating small water droplets and form clouds. The clouds get bigger as more water droplets cool and **condense**. The clouds hold the drops until they are large enough to fall to Earth as rain, hail, sleet or snow. This water fills dams, lakes and flows into creeks and rivers, or is trapped in ice, but eventually it flows back to the ocean where the water cycle starts again.

▼ The water cycle moves water around the planet and is powered by the heat of the sun. The ocean is a vital part of the Earth's water cycle, which provides important resources for life on Earth.

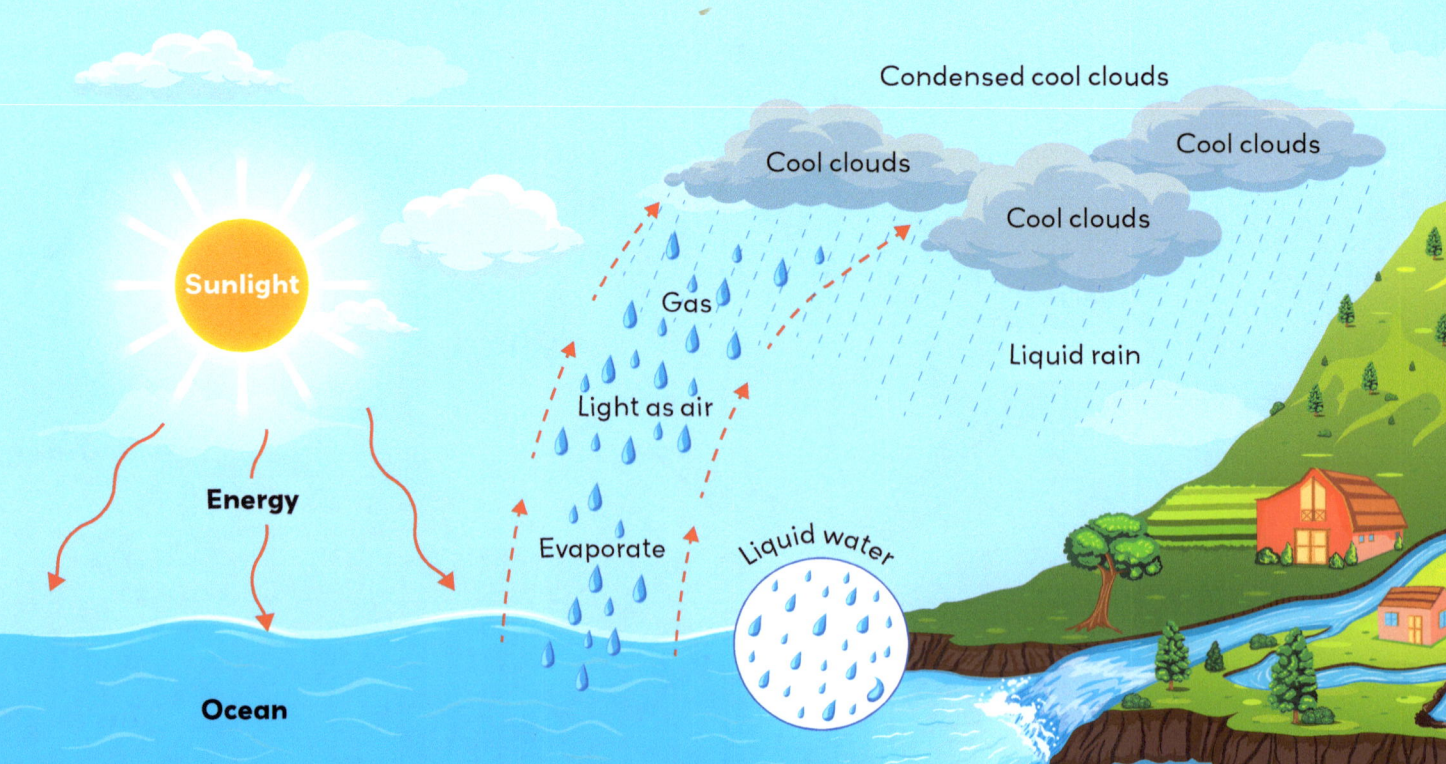

Chapter 1: The role of our oceans

Oceans help create the air we breathe

Water is alive! It's amazing to think that every drop of ocean water is teeming with over 1 million forms of **microscopic** life called **plankton**. Plankton live in the surface waters of the ocean. They are tiny and come in many different shapes and sizes. Some plankton are animals called zooplankton. Others are plant-like organisms called **phytoplankton**, which include **diatoms**, **cyanobacteria** and **algae**. Most phytoplankton are single cells.

Each tiny phytoplankton can create oxygen during **photosynthesis**. This is when light energy from the sun combines with carbon dioxide and water to produce food and oxygen. This happens in cells called **chloroplasts**, which are like solar panels, converting sunlight into energy. All plants and algae have chloroplasts that make simple sugars (carbohydrates) and oxygen from carbon dioxide and water, using the sun's energy.

Meet the phytoplankton, the oceans' oxygen-making mini factories. In the oceans, phytoplankton use sunlight energy to produce food for themselves and oxygen for all living things.

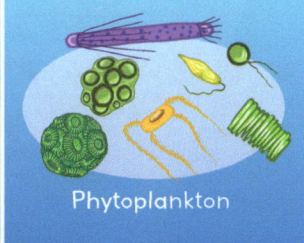

Sunlight   Carbon dioxide   Water   Phytoplankton   Oxygen   Carbon   Water
              CO_2 H_2O O_2 H_2O

Photosynthesis

Oceans of Plastic

As you take your next breath think about where that oxygen came from. Amazingly, one in every five breaths are made by marine phytoplankton! In the ocean, the photosynthesisers are seaweeds, algae and phytoplankton such as diatoms and cyanobacteria (blue-green **bacteria**). These tiny ocean dwelling organisms create over half the world's oxygen! They are the floating oxygen factories of the oceans.

Creature Feature

Exploding phytoplankton may create clouds

Some species of phytoplankton may help make clouds! Scientists are investigating how sea spray helps create clouds over oceans. They are studying a group of special microscopic phytoplankton – hard-shelled **coccolithophores**.

Coccolithophores are a phytoplankton. When seen under a microscope, they are incredibly beautiful. Their delicate hard shell is made of **calcium**, just like your teeth. Coccolithophores like *Emiliania huxleyi* can catch **viruses** that make them explode! Tiny parachute-shaped parts of their shell are tossed into the air with sea spray and bubbles. They are so light they can be carried up into the atmosphere where they help seed clouds. These ocean clouds become so large they reflect the sun's energy back out into space. This helps to make the ocean and our planet cooler.

Oceans and our climate

The carbon balance

The air we breathe is made up of a mixture of gases. It is roughly 78 per cent **nitrogen**, 21 per cent oxygen, and almost 1 per cent argon. Carbon dioxide is a **greenhouse gas**. There is only about 0.04 per cent of it in the atmosphere, and yet that tiny amount is helping to warm the planet. It is essential to have the right balance of these gases in the atmosphere. Too much carbon dioxide in the atmosphere and the planet warms. Too little and the planet cools. Just the right amount and we have the perfect temperature to support life on Earth.

Currently, our planet has the highest amount of carbon dioxide in the atmosphere in the last 800 000 years, because of human activities. We need to stop adding carbon dioxide and other greenhouse gases to the atmosphere and start removing them.

Storing carbon

The oceans help to remove **carbon** from the air. On the **coast**, plants like mangroves and seagrass take in carbon from the air and water. They store this carbon in their leaves, branches and root systems. This is called **blue carbon**. Under the water, seaweed and phytoplankton take in carbon dioxide and store it inside their cells. If the seaweed or phytoplankton is eaten, the carbon inside is passed to the next animal that eats it. When the seaweed or phytoplankton dies, it sinks down to the sea floor with the carbon inside. The carbon is safely stored in the **sediment** (sand, mud or silt) deep under the water, as a **carbon sink**. This keeps it out of the Earth's atmosphere.

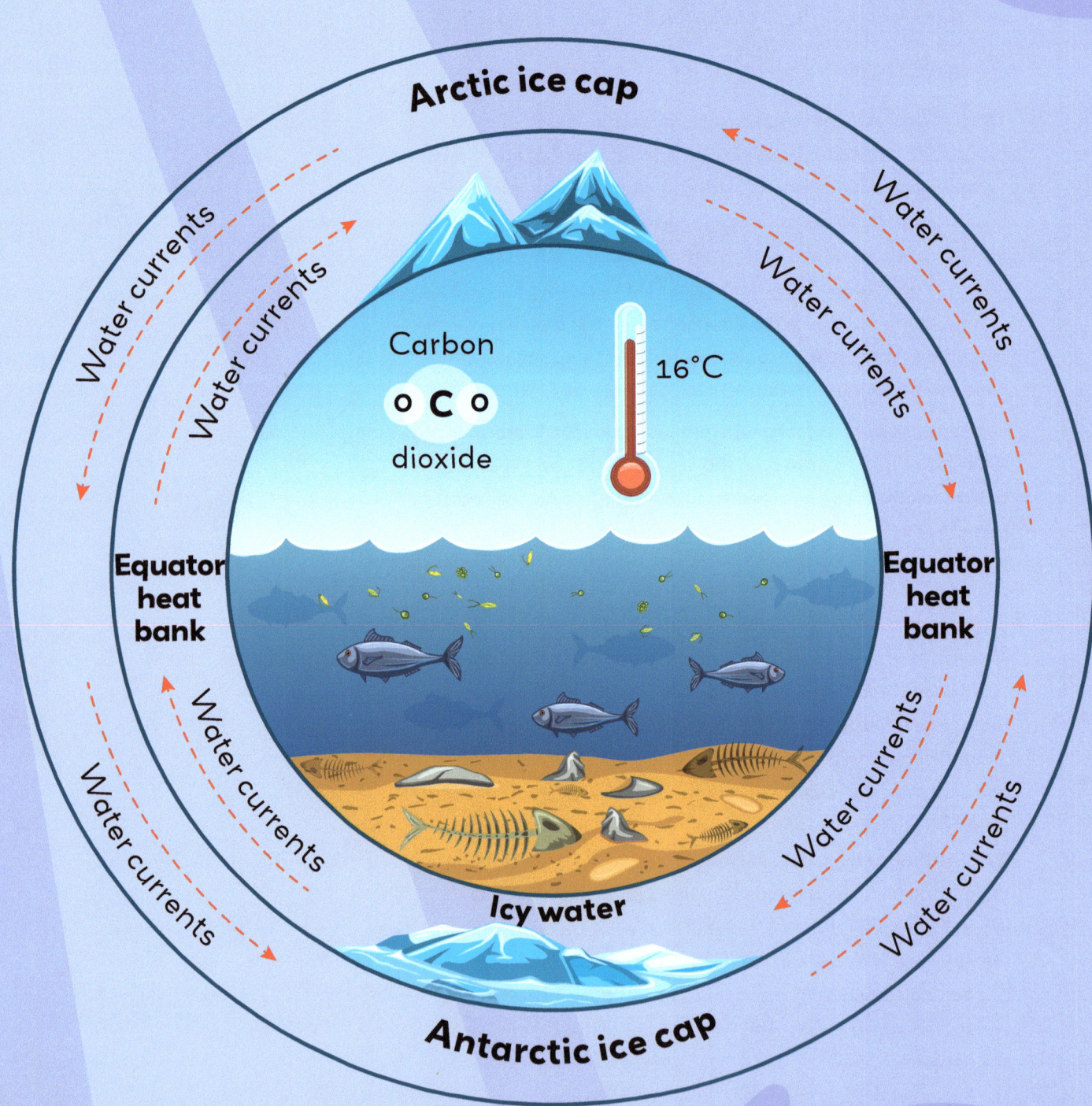

Chapter 1: The role of our oceans

Keeping it cool

The world's oceans can take in and release large amounts of heat energy without creating big changes in the temperature of the Earth. Have you ever run across burning hot sand into the cold ocean on a hot day? Then you'll know that the sand heats up faster than water. Sand grains are tiny and solid, heating up faster than water. As a liquid, water takes time to heat up. Water is great at trapping in the rays of sun, storing the heat and releasing it slowly. The temperature of the ocean water is important because it creates water currents and weather systems around the world, helping to control Earth's temperature.

Oceans help to stabilise the Earth's climate in several ways. Oceans are a carbon sink, storing carbon and keeping greenhouse gases out of the atmosphere. The ocean stores heat, helping to cool our planet. Oceans distribute heat and cold around the Earth through ocean currents, keeping the temperature stable and Earth just warm enough to support life on our planet.

Oceans of Plastic

It's all connected

Underneath the ocean there are large parts of sea floor waiting to be discovered! We have more detailed maps of the surface of Mars than of the sea floor. Each **continent** on Earth sits on a continental shelf. Australia's continental shelf extends to Tasmania in the south and New Guinea in the north. It creates a shallow sea that extends to the continental slope which drops steeply to the depths of the ocean floor. Australia's continental shelf sits on a **tectonic plate**. The Earth's crust consists of over 20 tectonic plates, with seven large plates under the continents and the Pacific Ocean. These tectonic plates also form the sea floor and **abyssal plain**.

Where two plates collided in the Western Pacific Ocean, they formed the Mariana Trench – the deepest part of the ocean. At its deepest point, the trench is 10 894 metres below the ocean surface, that's nearly 11 kilometres! The world's deepest canyon is called Challenger Deep, it is found at the southern end of the Mariana Trench.

How deep is the Mariana Trench? Imagine the highest mountain on Earth, Mount Everest, standing at a whopping 8848 metres (8.8 kilometres) above sea level. If we could move Mount Everest, we would easily fit it inside the Mariana Trench and there would still be 1600 metres (or 1.6 kilometres) of water above the highest peak!

▶ The Earth has one large interconnected ocean. The waters of the ocean continuously move around the planet. Mixing and stirring ocean waters renews food sources, provides transport for marine creatures and brings new weather to the land.

Chapter 1: The role of our oceans   19

Underwater mountain ranges

Hidden under the ocean is the longest mountain chain in the world! The mid-ocean ridge is 65 000 kilometres long! It is 10 times longer than the longest mountain range on land, the Andes in South America. The island of Mauna Kea, near Hawaii in the Atlantic Ocean, shows us a snow-covered mountain 4200 metres above the water. Below the water surface the mountain continues for another 5800 metres to the sea floor below.

When oceans thrive, we survive

Water, water everywhere, but not a drop to drink! Our oceans contain 97 per cent of the world's water, and it's salty. Let's investigate the world's freshwater supply. Imagine a bucket filled with 9 litres of water, this represents all the water of the world (including the oceans). Scoop out one-and-a-half cups of water from the bucket. This represents all of the freshwater found on the Earth! One cup holds the frozen water locked away in ice and ice caps (2 per cent). The remaining half a cup is the freshwater available for all living things to use and drink! This is the freshwater found in rivers, lakes, streams, in the atmosphere and underground (1 per cent). Water is precious, we can't survive without it.

Inside the oceans over 2 million species are found. Scientists estimate that 90 per cent are new species. Creatures that are yet to identified, leaving new discoveries waiting to be found. Healthy oceans are important for producing food and supporting marine species so they can thrive.

The ocean absorbs 90 per cent of the Earth's heat and stores over 30 per cent of carbon produced by humans. Without our oceans we would be living in much a warmer world!

Chapter 2

SLOW-MOTION OCEANS

Chapter 2: Slow-motion oceans 21

The movement of ocean currents is controlled by the biggest **natural** forces on Earth. These forces are the strong winds pushing across the ocean, the **rotation** of our planet, and the shape of the ocean floor. Together these forces create large slow-moving currents called ocean **gyres**.

Shaped by the land

Oceans have basins, like an enormous kitchen sink or bathroom basin. An ocean basin is surrounded by the coast, islands, reefs and the ocean floor. The ocean floor has hills, mountains, valleys and plains, just like those on dry land. An underwater landscape might have submerged mountain peaks, volcanic vents, deep **drop-off zones**, trenches and canyons. The ocean floor not only contains the water, it directs the movement of water. Its shape changes the way water moves over it.

   Imagine stirring a drink in a cup. A slow current begins to form as the liquid moves around the cup. Even when the spoon is taken out, the liquid keeps moving in a gentle spiral. This circular motion is called a gyre. If the cup was a rockpool, a square fish tank or a large swimming pool, its shape would change the way the water moves. Oceans have different shaped ocean floors and basins, that change the shape of the gyre current. Gyre currents can be forced into an oval shape or spread out into a big circular current.

Swirly sinks and slowly spinning ocean gyres

It is often said that the water in a sink or bathtub drains out in different directions, spinning down the plug hole either to the left or to the right depending on which part of the Earth you are on – but this isn't true. To see the effect in real life the amount of water needs to be huge! Ocean sized! It turns out that the way an ocean current moves depends both on the amount of water and the shape of the sea floor or ocean basin, as these affect how the current is squished or stretched out. The rotation of the Earth can also put a slow spin on things. These **elements** cause ocean gyres in the Northern **Hemisphere** to flow **clockwise** and in the Southern Hemisphere to flow **anticlockwise**.

Shaped by the land. A cup being slowly stirred creates a small current. In the ocean, the shape of the sea floor changes the shape of the gyre at the surface.

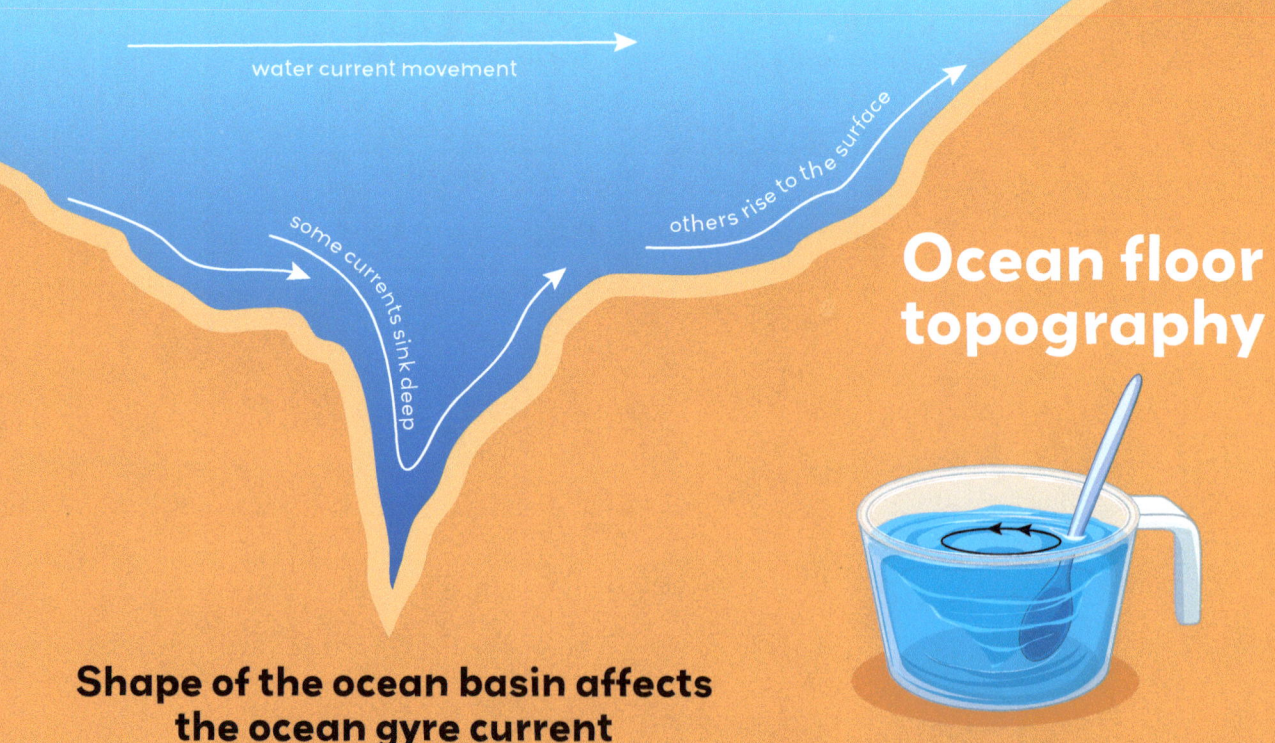

Ocean floor topography

Shape of the ocean basin affects the ocean gyre current

Chapter 2: Slow-motion oceans

Pushed by the wind

The ocean and the atmosphere are connected in powerful ways. Wind is the main force that creates and moves surface currents. Winds are caused by parts of the Earth heating up more than other parts.

The equator is an imaginary line around the widest part of the Earth. It divides the Earth into two halves: the Northern Hemisphere and the Southern Hemisphere. The Earth is tilted slightly on its axis, which creates the seasons. Around the equator, the weather is always warm and tropical. In the North Pole and South Pole, the weather is always cold.

When the sun shines on the equator, the air heats up and gently rises, like steam from a kettle. The air then heads towards the North and South poles. Here the air cools and falls back towards the surface of the Earth and blows back towards the equator. These giant air currents in the atmosphere circulate all around the globe between the equator and each of the poles, carrying moisture, heat and **pollution** with them.

These winds create **friction** between the air and water. The top layer of water is pushed forward by the wind, creating waves. As the top layer moves it pulls the layers of water beneath, creating the beginning of a large oceanic current. Not only is the wind at work, but the Earth's rotation is involved in the ocean gyre currents.

In a temperature race around the sky, cold air follows warm air and creates wind. As the winds slows it creates the movement of the waters of ocean gyres. Ocean gyres bring in floating objects, as they are caught up in the slow-turning waters.

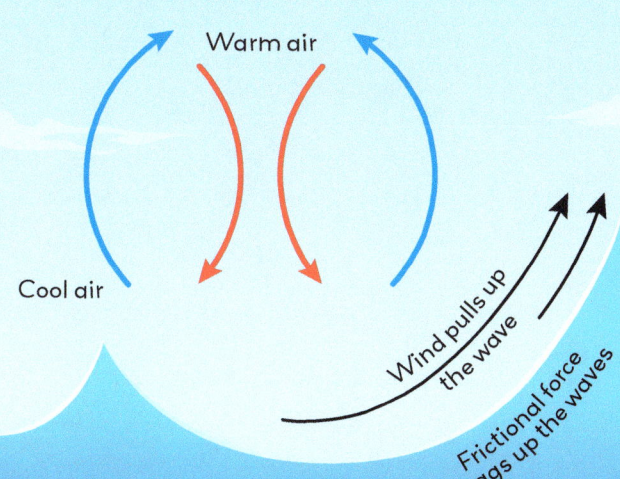

Push and pull of the ocean

Pulled by the planet

As you sit reading this page, you are spinning at 1600 kilometres an hour. It's hard to imagine, but that is how fast the Earth rotates. Because of the great size of the planet, the speed of its movement doesn't affect us, but it does affect the oceans.

The Earth's rotation affects air currents in the atmosphere and water currents in the ocean. If the planet didn't rotate, the air and ocean currents would move in straight lines from north to south between the warm equator and the cold poles.

Physical forces such as the **Coriolis Effect** and the **Ekman Spiral** also affect ocean currents. The Coriolis Effect occurs when wind pushes the surface water of the ocean. The Ekman Spiral pulls surface water down into the ocean depths in a spiral pattern.

▶ The Coriolis Effect is a force that affects an object that is moving over something that is turning or rotating. It causes wind and ocean currents to bend to the right (Northern Hemisphere) or left (Southern Hemisphere).

Chapter 2: Slow-motion oceans 25

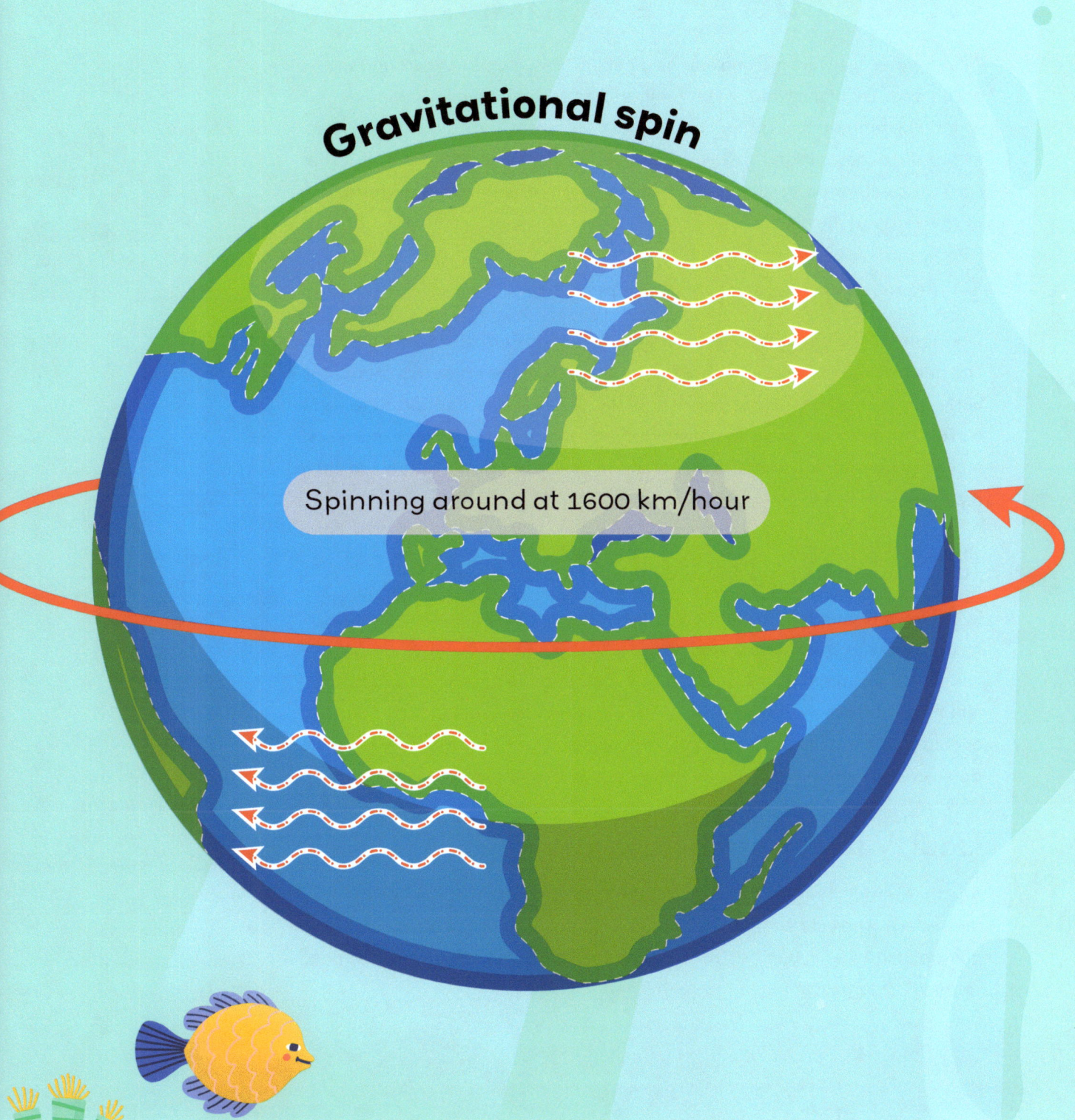

Ocean currents create a stir

Ocean water is always moving and never still. The currents flow around the ocean because of the wind, water temperature and the salinity (saltiness) of the water. The temperature difference between the warm and cold ocean water moves the ocean currents below, mixing the water in a continuous cycle. The currents can be slow, fast or circular. Currents move heat, nutrients (food) and oxygen around the planet.

Surface and deep currents

The warm surface currents carry warm water from the equator to the poles. The deep ocean currents carry cold water away from the poles to the equator. Surface currents move the upper layer of the ocean and last a short time. Tidal currents and rips are examples of short-lived surface currents. Deep currents move the deepest layers of the ocean and may take hundreds of years to circle the Earth.

Icy cold sinking currents

In the polar regions of the planet, less sunlight means colder oceans. Cold water is heavier than warm water, causing it to sink to the ocean floor. As colder water sinks, it pushes warmer water around the oceans. The Antarctic and the Arctic oceans have deep **convection currents** created by the sinking of cold water and the pushing up of warm water. These currents flow from the polar ice caps into the oceans, keeping them cool and stable.

Cool waters from below

An **upwelling current** pushes cold water from the bottom of the ocean to the surface. The cold water contains nutrients, feeding ocean life including, phytoplankton, krill, bait fish, tuna and dolphins. Upwelling currents support some of the largest marine **food webs** in the ocean.

▶ **Fast-flowing currents are water transport superhighways, moving water around the Earth. Cold water sinks and is pushed up over the deep-sea ridges, mixing the water and controlling the temperature of the Earth as it goes.**

Chapter 2: Slow-motion oceans 27

When nutrient-rich waters are brought up into warmer sunlight, the microscopic algae in the phytoplankton multiply quickly, producing **algae blooms**, covering the ocean surface. Some algae blooms are big enough to be seen by satellites in space!

Quick currents on the move

The Antarctic Circumpolar Current is the only current that flows right around the Earth. It surrounds Antarctica and is the coldest current of all. It keeps warmer waters away from Antarctica, helping to keep it icy cold.

The Leeuwin Current is the longest current in the world! It flows for over 5000 kilometres down the coast of Western Australia, then along the coast of South Australia into the Great Australian Bight. It brings warm water all the way to the Tasman Sea and the Southern Ocean.

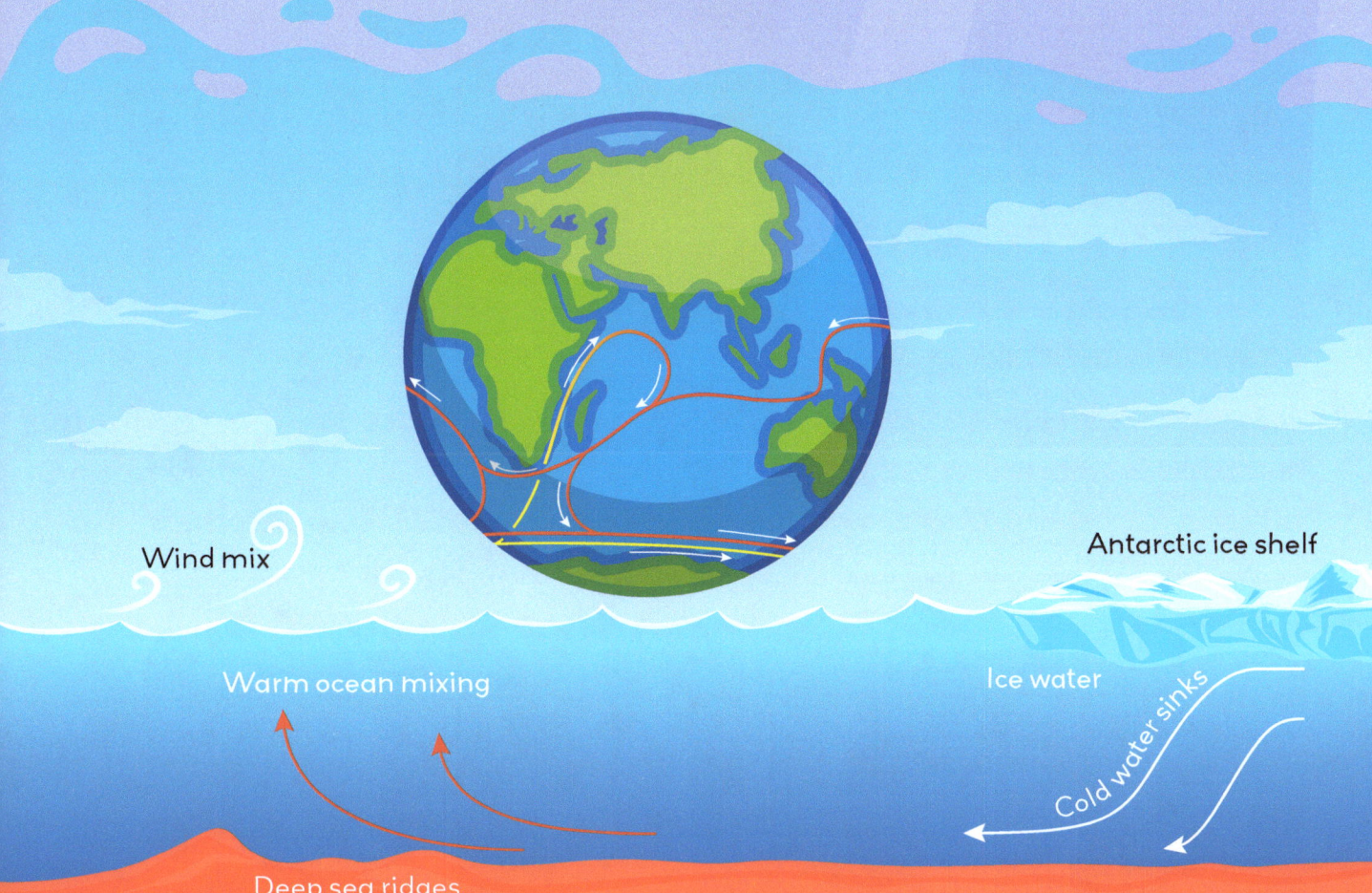

Oceans of Plastic

The Indonesian Through Flow is a system of currents that carry water west from the Pacific to the Indian Ocean, past the Indonesian islands and into the Leeuwin Current. It is the only place in the world where warm, tropical water flows from ocean to ocean. The warm water held in the currents and moisture in the atmosphere are important to global weather patterns.

The East Australian Current is a large, warm, productive current off Australia. It brings warm water from the tropical regions of the Coral Sea down along the coast of Australia to the Tasman Sea. This current is so fast, it moves a massive 35 million litres of water per second! Just imagine 14 000 Olympic-sized swimming pools of water moving every second in this current. **Oceanographers** measured the East Australian Current at 100 kilometres wide and 500 metres deep.

Massive marine mammal migration

On an epic ocean **migration** journey, humpback whales swim over 10 000 kilometres each year! In late summer humpback whales (*Megaptera novaeangliae*) leave their cold-water feeding grounds near Antarctica in the Southern Ocean. Pods of humpback whales swim against ocean currents surrounding Australia to reach their warm-water breeding areas. Some whales swim up the East Australian Current, while others swim against the Leeuwin Current off Western Australia. The whales **migrate** to give birth to their young calves in warm oceans. These waters are perfect for saving energy and putting on weight. The mother whales feed their babies over 250 litres of milk a day, to prepare them for the return to their feeding grounds in Antarctica.

Chapter 2: Slow-motion oceans

Great ocean gyres

There are five great gyres on Earth. The Atlantic Ocean and the Pacific Ocean both have two ocean gyres each. They are found in the north and south areas of their oceans. The Indian Ocean has one large gyre. Gyres also form in cold polar oceans. The Alaskan Current and the Norwegian Current are found in the Northern Hemisphere. The Weddell Gyre and Ross Gyre are found in the Southern Hemisphere. The northern Pacific Ocean Gyre is the largest on the planet. The Indian Ocean Gyre is the second largest.

These gyres all differ in shape, speed, temperature and size. The waters that form the gyre can be icy cold, cold or warm. For this reason, oceanographers group gyres into different categories: **subpolar**, **subtropical** and tropical.

How is an ocean gyre made? Ocean gyres are made by the Earth's natural forces: they are pushed by the wind, shaped by the land and pulled by the planet. Fast-moving ocean water slows down as it reaches the equator. The warm winds push the water in a spiral movement. The Earth's forces become the power source of the gyre's continual movement.

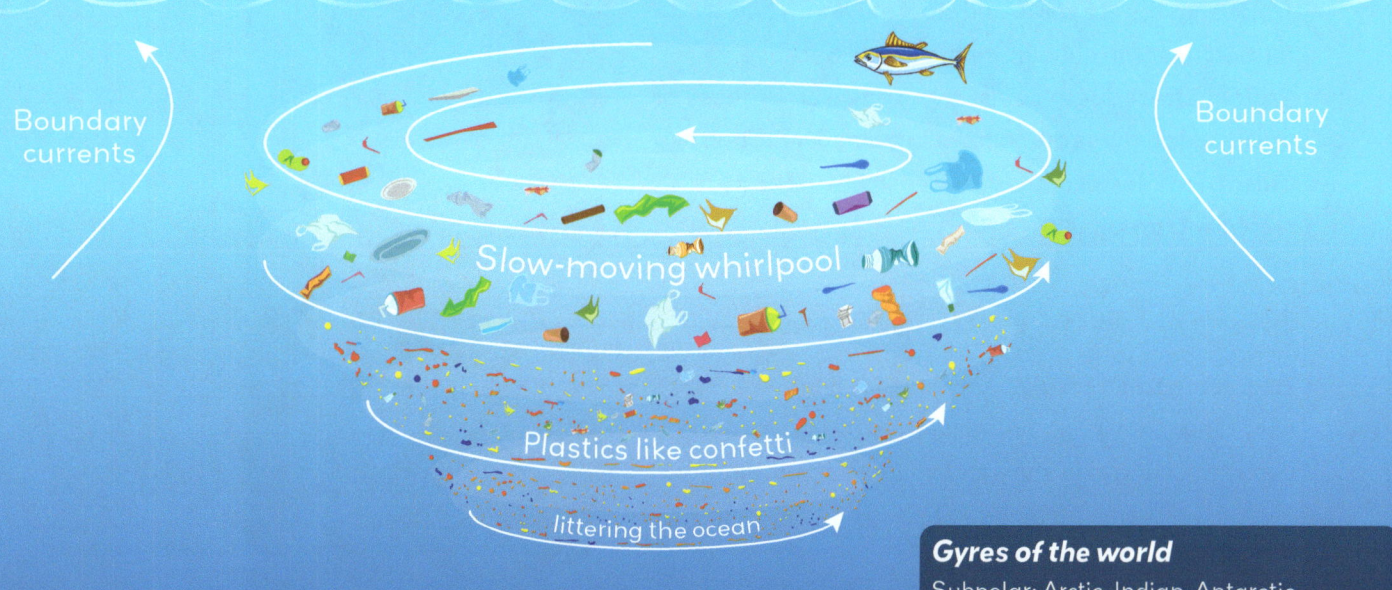

Ocean gyres

Boundary currents

Slow-moving whirlpool

Plastics like confetti

littering the ocean

Boundary currents

Gyres of the world
Subpolar: Arctic, Indian, Antarctic
Subtropical: North Atlantic, South Atlantic
Tropical: North Pacific, South Pacific

Subpolar gyres

Subpolar gyres carry icy water around Antarctica in the Southern Ocean and around the Arctic seas. The waters of subpolar gyres are so cold they contain icebergs. They are also rich in nutrients brought up to the surface from deep below. These nutrients feed the entire ecosystem of polar marine animals that live there.

Subtropical gyres

Subtropical gyres are the largest ocean gyres. They are found in the warmer ocean waters of the Pacific, Indian and Atlantic oceans. The outer edges of the gyres are like underwater ocean highways, used by marine creatures, such as whales, to move around the planet. These are called boundary currents.

Tropical gyres

Tropical gyres are warm and slow moving. They are formed near the equator by the winds because the Coriolis Effect doesn't exist at the equator. Because of this, tropical gyres don't move in a circular motion like other gyres. Instead, they flow east to west and are stable and predictable.

Break-away eddies

Eddies are small circular currents that don't last for very long. They bring nutrients from the deep to the surface. Changes in wind and water temperature can create them and they can form off to the side of powerful boundary currents.

Duck-spill!

In 1992 a shipping container full of rubber ducks fell overboard, spilling 28 000 ducks into the northern Pacific Ocean! The ducks floated on the currents and washed up on beaches all over the world. This ocean-sized rubber duck event helped us learn more about the way the ocean currents move, by seeing how far and wide the ducks travelled. Keep an eye on your rubber duckie, in case it is planning an ocean escape!

Chapter 3

CATCHING A CURRENT

Ocean drifters

Ocean currents create water transport systems for marine life. The currents assist marine creatures to navigate across oceans to feed and to find mates or new places to live. Marine turtles use currents to help them swim long distances. Why not catch a ride on the biggest currents in the ocean to quickly reach your destination?

Creature Feature

Marine leatherback turtles

Going with the flow on the open ocean

Marine leatherback turtles (*Dermochelys coriacea*) are one of the ocean creatures that go with the flow. The turtles use ocean currents to travel the world. It's a great energy saving idea when your main food source of jellyfish is made of 95 per cent water.

When turtles drift on the currents, they take in all types of information about marine habitats. Turtles remember their favourite eating spots like seagrass meadows or algae-filled reefs. Turtles drift on currents in suitable habitat areas where they find food and the water temperature is warm. A turtle will actively swim out of unsuitable habitats with cooler water or areas with limited food.

No matter how far they travel, female turtles always return to the same beach on which they hatched. Leatherback turtles return when they are ready to breed at 15–25 years old. Then the females come ashore to lay their eggs deep in the sand. Female leatherback turtles nest every 2–5 years. Between nesting they spend their time exploring the ocean looking for food, finding mates and using the currents to navigate across the ocean. The male turtles spend their time cruising the ocean currents and never return to the beach once hatched.

Chapter 3: Catching a current

SCIENCE IN ACTION

Travelling turtles follow invisible magnetic fields around the oceans

Scientists have discovered that turtles use the Earth's **magnetic field** to navigate around the ocean. We use the Earth's magnetic field when we use a compass. A magnetic field is the area around a magnet in which there is magnetic force. The Earth is like a giant magnet with its own magnetic field. Magnets (and the Earth) have a north and south pole.

Marine biologists say the first few years of a turtle's life are 'the lost years' as they are not sure where hatchling turtles go exactly. In a quest to find out where sea turtles travel, biologists attached tiny tracking tags on the shells of day-old hatchlings. Scientists think that turtles use the Earth's magnetic field like a **Global Positioning System (GPS)** to help them find their way. The turtles develop a sensory map of the oceans, noting good food spots and currents to use when returning to nesting areas. When the scientists collect the information from the tracking tags, they can see the currents that the turtles used. The information tells them where they drift and when they are actively swimming. Scientists have found there are common paths between nesting and feeding areas. These are called migration corridors.

Floating lizards on a coconut raft

In an ocean gyre, currents carry anything that floats, such as driftwood, coconut shells, seaweed and plastic. Wild storms can blow trees like coconut palms into the ocean, and floating items can become accidental **rafts**. Land-based animals can become passengers on unplanned ocean voyages. Lizards such as iguanas have been found on distant islands, drifting onto the beaches on fallen coconuts or trees.

Volcanic rock rafts

Bubble, rock and roll! Active underwater volcanos have been erupting for hundreds of millions of years, helping to transport marine life around the oceans. When underwater sea vents or volcanos erupt, they can spill out **lava** into the ocean. The lava can form floating mats or rafts of volcanic **pumice**. Pumice is a lightweight, bubble-filled rock that floats in water. It is formed when frothy **magma** hits the water and cools fast, trapping air bubbles inside.

▼

Ocean drifters catch a ride in an ocean current. Turtles, limpets and lizards can all use the ocean to move around, as babies, adults or even as stowaways.

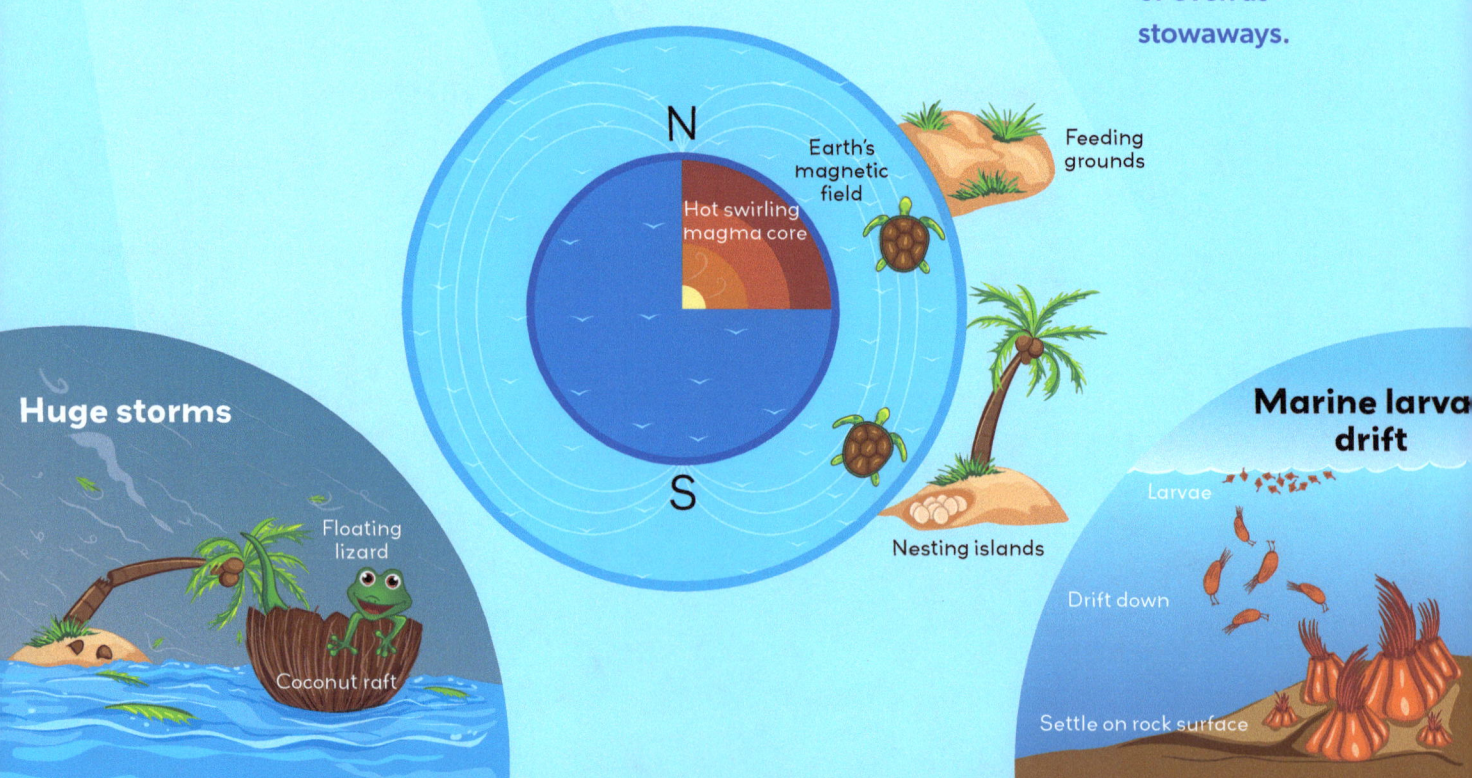

Huge storms — Floating lizard — Coconut raft

Hot swirling magma core — Earth's magnetic field — Feeding grounds — Nesting islands

Marine larva drift — Larvae — Drift down — Settle on rock surface

Chapter 3: Catching a current

Spreading larvae around the ocean

As a great survival plan, ocean species send out their young (**larvae**) on ocean currents! Sea creatures such as sea snails, jellyfish, sea anemones, fan worms and coral release millions of eggs and sperm into the water. This is called **broadcast spawning**. The eggs and sperm float to the surface of the ocean where they mix and the fertilised eggs become larvae. As the larvae grow, they float in the sea as zooplankton and provide food for many other animals. If the larvae aren't eaten, they drift down and settle on the sea floor – on rocks, sand or a coral reef – and make their home.

Once a year on a full moon a special **synchronised** event happens in the Great Barrier Reef. Corals release tiny egg and sperm bundles as spawn into the water. They create an amazing event that looks like a colourful underwater snowstorm that can last for a week or more.

Mega pumice sea rafts

In 2019 a mega pumice raft was created by a submarine volcanic eruption near Tonga in the Pacific Ocean. The pumice raft spread out over 200 square kilometres (that's the size of Port Phillip Bay in Victoria, Australia!). Three weeks later the currents had spread the raft over 3000 square kilometres.

Each piece of pumice can become a floating home, a vehicle for living things to attach to and be transported over thousands of kilometres away within a few months. **Geochemical scientists** have found that large rafts of pumice can transport species over 30 kilometres each day. The pumice rafts can help living things to cross deep oceans that would normally act as a **geographical barrier**. Pumice helps to transport corals, barnacles, anemones, crabs, molluscs and other sea life to new areas. The pumice can also be a place for marine pests to hitch a ride, and if not monitored can become a problem.

Creature Feature

A limpet's life

Many marine creatures are **sedentary**. This means they don't move around much. A limpet (*Cellana tramoserica*) is a small marine snail. Limpets live their entire life on one rock! Limpets can live to 20 years of age. As baby limpets (larvae), they spend a few days floating about in ocean currents then sink down to a new place. Here they find their rock, settle in and grow. This is an excellent strategy for limpets and other sea snails. It helps them find mates and spread out their young, which reduces competition for food and space.

TRACEY GRAY

◀ Limpet larvae are transported on currents to new areas. They settle into crevices in rockpools, where they grow and live. The limpet shell protects and helps them to survive in tidal rockpools.

Chapter 4

GREAT OCEANS! IT'S A GARBAGE PATCH!

Caught up in the current

Plastic is not a natural part of the ocean. Humans are the only creatures that make and use plastic. Each year more than 8–10 million tonnes of our plastic are entering the world's oceans. This plastic is being blown into the sea by wind, washed into rivers or dropped into the ocean. Once in the ocean these plastics can be washed back onto shore or carried by ocean currents.

80% Land — Transported by rivers, Blown by wind
20% Ships — Fishing gear

◀ Look where all the plastic rubbish comes from! We find 80 per cent of ocean rubbish comes from land and 20 per cent from fishing and ships. The rubbish coming from land is mainly from packaging, while fishing gear is lost from boats and ships.

What a lot of ocean rubbish

Every year 8–10 million tonnes of plastic end up in the world's oceans. That's equal to one rubbish truck full of plastics entering the oceans, every minute of every day!

It's a plastic soup out there

Imagine you're sailing home from Hawaii in a yacht. After a week of seriously big waves, you decide to take a short cut across the Pacific Ocean. You find yourself in an eerily quiet place. There is not a breath of wind, and you are far from land. In the water you notice a faded blue bottle top, a plastic bag, a plastic drink bottle – there are tiny plastic pieces everywhere. You've entered the waters of the Pacific gyre, and you are stuck in the biggest floating garbage patch in the world!

In 1997, Captain Charles Moore, an oceanographer, was alarmed when he found a huge patch of plastic-filled water out in the middle of the Pacific Ocean. Fishing nets, toothbrushes, bottle tops, water bottles and plastic bags were easy to recognise. Other smaller pieces of plastic were broken up, which he described as confetti or cupcake sprinkles. These **fragments** of plastic float just below the surface of the ocean waters. Captain Moore named the area the '**Great Pacific Garbage Patch**'.

The Great Pacific Garbage Patch was formed when ocean currents slowed and brought in floating items. The swirling motion of the ocean creates the perfect place for plastic pieces to collect in an underwater plastic soup.

Oceans of Plastic

When Captain Moore returned home, he told people about the plastic pollution in the oceans. News of the Great Pacific Garbage Patch spread around the world, and scientific voyages and **research** scientists started to uncover a global environmental problem. We need to think about what really happens when we throw away our plastic toothbrushes, pens, bags and drink bottles. We like to think they have gone away forever, but if plastic isn't disposed of correctly, it can end up in the ocean.

How big is the Great Pacific Garbage Patch?

The Great Pacific Garbage Patch is described as being twice the size of Texas in America, as big as Queensland in Australia or three times the size of France in Europe. It is 1.6 million square kilometres and growing. The plastic in the Great Pacific Garbage Patch is estimated to weigh more than 43 000 cars! The Great Pacific Garbage Patch holds over 1.8 trillion pieces of plastic, floating beneath the surface. If we divided up the plastic pieces evenly, between everyone on the planet, we would each have 250 pieces. This is just the start of the plastic problem, with four more big ocean gyres with plastic in their waters.

Lurking beneath the surface

The plastic found at the surface of the ocean is only the start of the plastic story. Plastic is finding its way to the deepest parts of the ocean. A deep-water submarine called the Okeanos Explorer identified a plastic bag in the Mariana Trench at 10 975 metres deep. After viewing over 5000 hours of underwater video collected by the submarine, scientists found plastics in over 50 per cent of the video. Scientists have been investigating ocean plastics to understand how much plastic is out there. They have learned that there is more plastic in our oceans than ever before and it's changing our oceans forever.

▶ Plastic, plastic everywhere! The plastics in the ocean are suspended in the water, floating and moving with the currents. Some plastics sink, others remain on the surface.

TANGAROA BLUE FOUNDATION

Chapter 4: Great oceans! It's a garbage patch! | 41

Plastic stars

Scientists estimate that a massive 5.5 trillion pieces of plastic are floating in the world's oceans. There are more pieces of plastic in the ocean than visible stars in the Milky Way.

Plastic not so fantastic

Did you know that plastic was created to replace ivory from elephant tusks? Elephants were being slaughtered to make ivory billiard balls, so in 1869 a New York business offered a $US10 000 reward to make an alternative to ivory. The first plastic was made with cotton and camphor oil. It could be moulded into many shapes and replaced ivory, tortoiseshell, bone, tusk and horn. The earliest form of plastic was made to help save wildlife – but now it's having the opposite effect!

By the 1960s, plastic had changed to a strong and lightweight product. Plastic replaced materials like glass, ceramics and **metal**. It was cheap to make, easy to use, light, hard to break and it cost less to transport.

People became hooked on plastic, and more and more disposable items were produced: plastic straws, cutlery, crockery, toys, bottles, crates, pots, radios ... The invention was meant to make our lives easier. Don't wash dishes – just throw them away! Many products were designed to be used once, then thrown away. The idea of **single-use** plastics was born. In 60 years, over 8.3 billion tonnes of plastic have been created, and every day more is made!

Not all plastics are bad; we need plastics for many purposes including medical treatments. These plastics are designed for single use and can't be reused safely. The problem with single-use plastic is how much is being made and how we choose to dispose of it. Each year 380 million tonnes of plastic are made. Over 50 per cent are single-use plastics! Used for only a short time, the impact will last a very long time.

Chapter 4: Great oceans! It's a garbage patch!   43

Going to pieces

The plastic that we use every day does not break down in nature like wood, cotton or paper. When plastic is exposed to natural forces like sunlight and wave action it breaks up into smaller plastic pieces. One plastic object can become millions of tiny plastic particles. In laboratory experiments, scientists found that an average plastic bag could break up into over 20 million plastic particles! That's only one plastic carry bag, made of two sheets of soft plastic. What a big impact one bag can have on the marine environment!

Cracking up the plastic

When hard plastic enters the ocean, it breaks into smaller fragments. The plastic changes as it reacts with the seawater. Cracks start appearing. The seawater soaks into and leaks out of the plastic pieces. As the plastic **weathers** in the ocean, it can change its outer texture from smooth to rough, and its size, colour, shape and ability to float.

TRACEY GRAY

This collection of ocean-washed plastics shows cracks beginning to form. After being in the ocean the plastics become weathered, as they are washed in the waves, rubbed by sand or rocks, lived on by microscopic life or exposed to the sun.

The weathering of plastics

If you leave your things outside in the weather for a few weeks or months they begin to change. They may fade, crack and look a little different. These changes are because of **weathering**. Let's investigate how weathering happens to plastic in the ocean:

- Light: The longer plastic is exposed to sunlight, the harder and more brittle it becomes. Sunlight can form small cracks that can make the plastic break up. Scientists call this **photodegradation** (photo = sun, degradation = break up).

- Water: In the ocean, chemicals from plastic are released into the water. Plastic also takes in chemicals from the surrounding water. Over time, plastic can become concentrated pieces of pollution.

- Living things: Microscopic living things like bacteria and algae attach to the surface of the plastic. The **microbes** affect the ability for objects to float.

- Heat: Most plastics start off floating in the ocean. Plastic can be 40–60 per cent lighter than saltwater, causing it to float on the surface where it is exposed to sunlight. Some coloured plastics have sunlight stabilisers, which act as a sunscreen, slowing the break-up of the plastic.

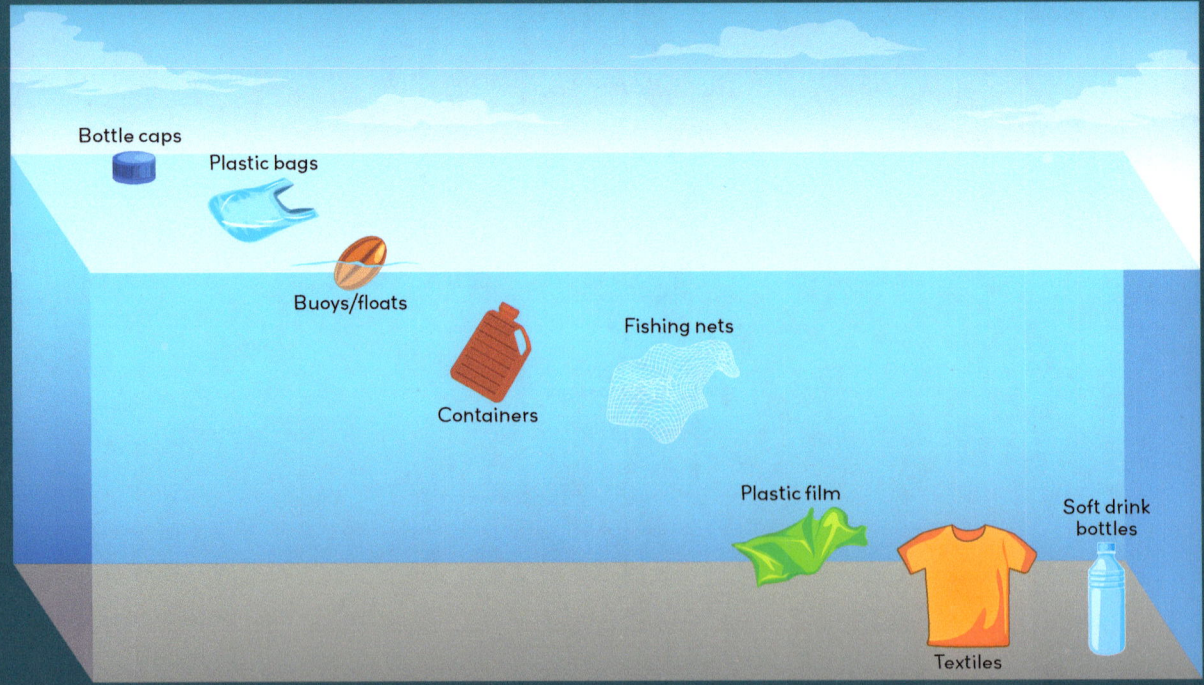

 Which plastics float and which sink in seawater?

The plastisphere

Life on the surface of the Earth is called the biosphere. Life on the surface of ocean plastic is called the **plastisphere**. To understand the plastisphere we have to think on a really small (micro) scale. In the sea there are millions of microbes ready to attach onto the plastic pieces like a thin **biofilm**. Once attached the microbes turn the plastic into a liveable habitat. The plastic surface needs to be slightly weathered for the micro community to start growing.

First the sunlight-seeking algae attach and start growing. Then the microbes that graze on algae arrive. Soon after, the **predators** and **decomposers** settle in. It is estimated that over 1000 kinds of microbes can be living on a single piece of plastic that is only 5 millimetres in size!

As the community of the plastisphere grows, something fascinating happens: the faster algae and bacteria grow on the surface of the plastic the heavier it becomes. The microscopic life changes the weight of the plastic, making it heavier, so it sinks down in the water. Small plastic pieces can reach their deepest point at midday when sunlight is the brightest. As night-time comes the plastic floats back to the surface. This movement of small pieces of plastic up and down in the water happens every day. It may go on for weeks or months depending on the type of plastic and where it is found in the ocean, until eventually the plastic piece sinks forever.

The plastisphere: a new floating home. Plastic pieces like lids are **colonised** by microbes, algae and **invertebrates** forming a living platform. The plastic sinks and rises in the water as the weight of the microbes grows.

Plastic bobbing around

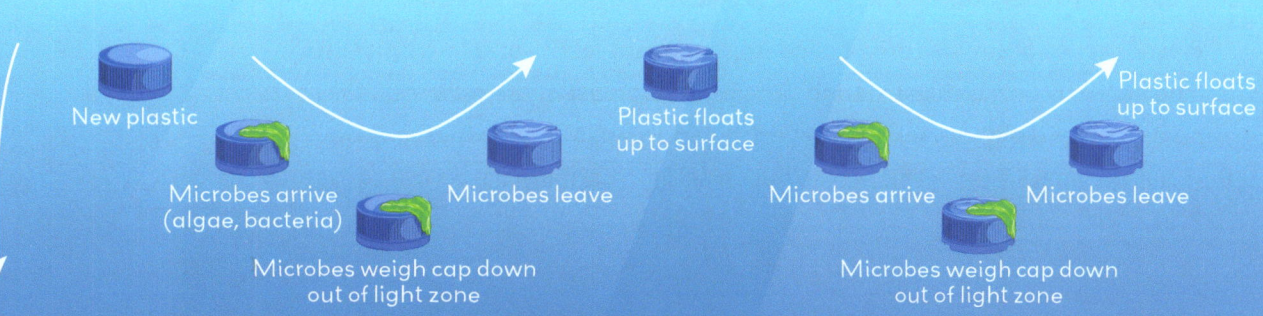

How many pieces of plastic in the ocean?

The Ocean CleanUp Foundation conducted the largest scientific survey of plastic in the Great Pacific Garbage Patch. In 2015, a fleet of 30 ships pulled over 650 nets through the water to collect floating plastic. They found over 1.7 trillion items of plastic, from small fragments to large items such as fishing nets, plastic drums and bottles. They found plastic **waste** dating back to 1977 – these items had been in the ocean for nearly 40 years!

Marine litter comes in all shapes and sizes.

Making the invisible plastics visible

When it comes to ocean plastic, size matters. To help sort out the plastic pieces they are grouped into different sizes, from **microplastics** to megaplastics.

The super-invisible plastics

Nanoplastics are between 1000th and 1 000 000th of a millimetre in size. These are the smallest of the small. We need a powerful microscope to see them, and yet they are everywhere. They are found in drinking water, the air we breathe, the food we eat and of course in the ocean.

Nanoplastics are added to products such as cosmetics and washing powders. **Microfibres** are nanoplastics. Every time we wash clothes made from plastic fabrics like polar fleece, the microfibres are released from the fabric. These human-made materials are flushed from the washing machine into the wastewater and eventually out to sea.

Plastic pieces of any size are of concern, but nanoplastics and microplastic can be eaten by our simplest marine species. Microplastics are now found in zooplankton and phytoplankton floating in the ocean. Microplastics may be tiny, but they pack a powerful plastic punch and are harming life on our planet.

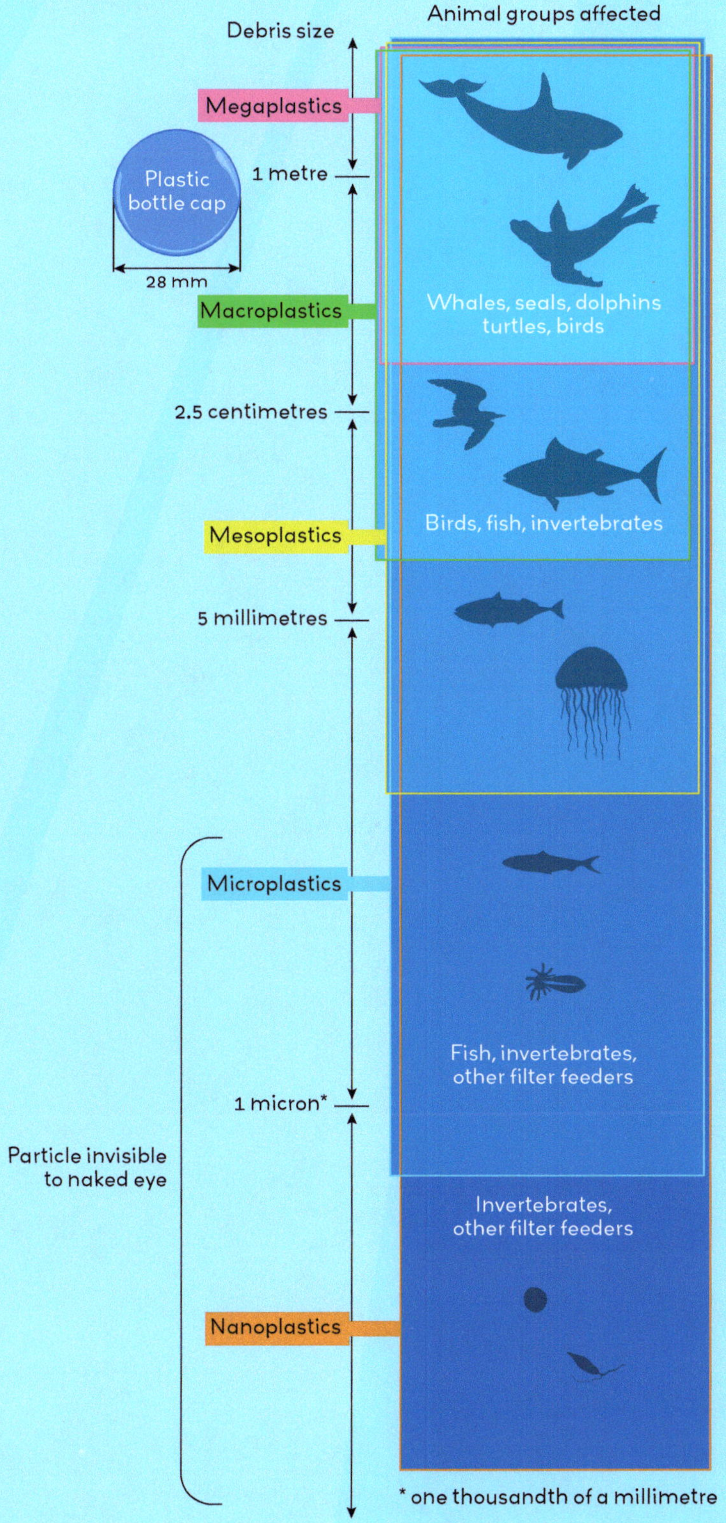

Chapter 4: Great oceans! It's a garbage patch!   47

Debris size | **Animal groups affected**

- Megaplastics — 1 metre (Plastic bottle cap, 28 mm)
- Macroplastics — 2.5 centimetres — Whales, seals, dolphins, turtles, birds
- Mesoplastics — 5 millimetres — Birds, fish, invertebrates
- Microplastics — 1 micron* — Fish, invertebrates, other filter feeders
- Nanoplastics — Invertebrates, other filter feeders

Particle invisible to naked eye

* one thousandth of a millimetre

TRACEY GRAY

▲ **Plastisphere on beach-washed plastics.** Look closely at the surface of the red piece of plastic and you can see the white outer casing of a tube worm. Sometimes marine creatures such as tube worms, barnacles or anemones attach to plastics. These creatures make use of the floating objects just like the microscopic plastisphere community.

Bottle build-up

What a lot of plastic! Over 1 million plastic water bottles are purchased every minute of every day. Our thirst for water is damaging our oceans, with all the disposable plastic. Re-think your next drink and refill a reusable bottle.

Chapter 5

A LIFETIME OF PLASTIC

Prehistoric past

Do you know how old plastic is? Plastic is made from plants, animals, plankton and algae that lived on the Earth or floated in the oceans over 150 million years ago!

In the ocean, living things like plankton make and store their own carbon. When plankton die, they drift down and settle on the sea floor. Here they are covered by thick layers of sand and sediment. Over a really, really long time, these cells change into a sticky, oily sludge, rich in carbon. These ocean fossils form oil and gas.

On land a similar thing happens. As carbon-storing plants and animals die, they are covered by sand, mud and soil sediments. Over time, these cells also form into oil, coal and gas. These are called **fossil fuels**. It takes millions of years for living things to become a fossil fuel!

Humans find and remove the fossil fuels of coal, oil or gas, and use it as a fuel. We use these fuels to power our world, drive our cars and make products like plastic.

Super strong and flexible bonds

Oil is a fossil fuel, and the ancient carbon in it is used to make different types of plastic. The plastic can be strong and hard, soft and squishy, or bendable and flexible. Just about anything can be made from plastic.

The molecules in plastic are connected by strong carbon bonds. These bonds hold together for years, which is excellent when we need a plastic container to hold tomato sauce, mayonnaise or chocolate topping. Our kitchen cupboards would become very messy places if the plastic bonds broke apart quickly, leaking out the liquids inside before we had time to use them.

Plastic becomes a problem when the container is no longer needed. When the plastic is thrown out, the bonds still hold. The food waste begins to rot away inside but the plastic stays in shape. This is why recycling is important. By melting down and reusing the plastic, we can transform it into a new product. Recycling stops plastic becoming waste on the land or in the oceans.

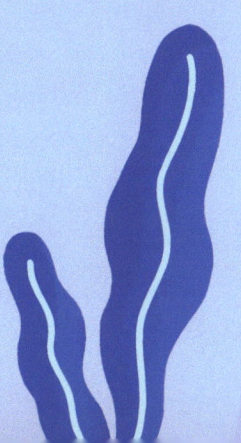

Oceans of Plastic

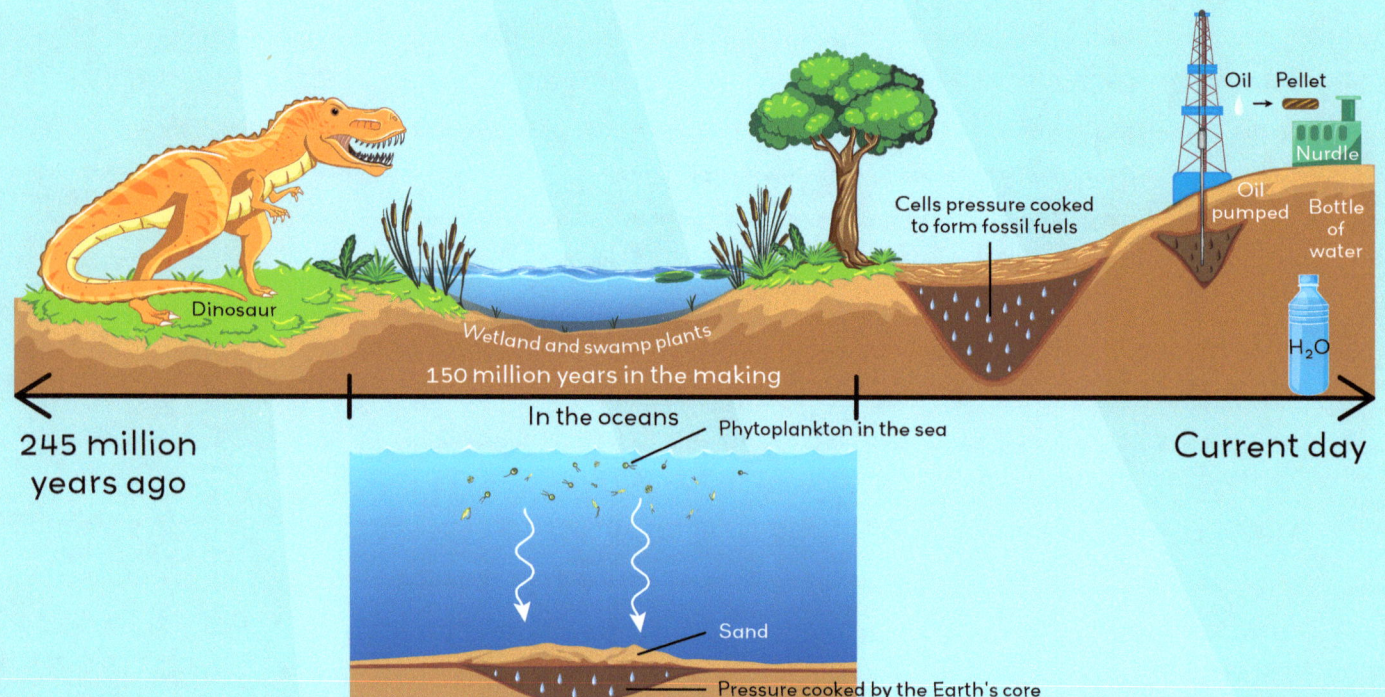

▲ The evolution of a plastic bottle. Fresh from the dinosaurs and ancient phytoplankton to perfectly cooked fossil fuels. Under the sea and soil, oil is formed over 150 million years. To make a plastic bottle the oil is changed into plastic pellets. The pellets are melted and reshaped into a new plastic bottle.

Plastics and the microbes

If plastic comes from oil created by the remains of creatures that lived millions of years ago, you may think that it can be broken down easily. But it's not as easy as it seems because the oil in plastic has changed during manufacturing. Plastic is made of carbon mixed with other chemicals to create long, strong products that won't break apart. This means they are harder for nature to break apart. In nature, microbes are powerhouse super-munchers of materials, but they need the right conditions to survive. So, the place where plastic ends up is important if microbes are to eat it.

Mighty land-loving microbes

On land, microbes like bacteria get to work by breaking down the **organic** carbon-based things that are easy to **decompose**, like food, paper packaging or wooden containers. When the microbes reach plastic, **digesting** it is much harder. Think of a juice box: microbes can get in and consume the left-over juice quickly, but the plastic packaging takes so much more time! They usually give up and move onto something faster to eat.

The lifespan of plastic is tested by exposing it to microbes like bacteria, **fungi** and algae to see if they can break it apart. Most microbes don't instantly recognise plastic as a natural food source. They have not **evolved** with the human-made plastic. Those long, strong **polymer** chains are hard to break.

Marvellous marine microbes

There are pit-forming bacteria species that are able to chew into the surface of plastics. These species may contribute to the breakdown of plastics, and it is hoped that more species can be found. But there are trillions of plastic pieces in the ocean, spread over large areas, so we can't just leave it up to microbes to sort out our plastic mess. We need to help stop the plastics getting into the oceans to help out the marine microbes!

Sorting out the plastics

Bread tags, bottles, bottle caps, cotton-bud sticks, plastic tags on clothing, and toothbrushes are all made of different types of plastic. Many plastic items have a plastic symbol stamped on them – a triangle with a number from one to seven. This symbol tells us if the plastic can be **recycled**. Most hard plastics are numbered 1 to 7 and can be recycled, if your local council recycles all types of plastic. The most common recycled plastic is clear plastic made of PET (number 1). Some plastics like bread tags are made of polystyrene and can't be recycled. Always check the number of the plastic and see if it can be recycled.

Nurdles in the ocean

A **nurdle** is a small, hard plastic pellet that is melted down to make plastic products. The pellets are the same size as a grain of rice, but rounder, like a lentil. Nurdles are a microplastic.

How many nurdles does it take to make a bottle?

It takes around 600 nurdles to make a 600 ml bottle. Over 1 million plastic bottles are used every minute on the planet! That makes a whopping 1.3 billion bottles used each day. This means that a massive 780 billion nurdles are needed to make the 1.3 billion bottles used every day! That's a lot of nurdles, but it's only those used for clear plastic bottles. It doesn't include all the other plastic products, such as food containers, plastic lids and clear plastic wraps, created every day across the world.

▲ Nurdles of all different shapes and sizes are used to make plastic products. These nurdles have been collected off a beach. Nurdles are small microplastics almost impossible to pick out of the sand.

▲ As small as a lentil, it takes a whole lot of nurdles to make one plastic product. Imagine how many nurdles are needed to make the plastic products the world uses every day. The work of Nurdlers involves counting the microplastics to add into marine **databases**.

Chapter 5: A lifetime of plastic

Can you outlive your lunchbox?

Is it possible to outlive the items inside your lunchbox? It is if your lunchbox is filled with nude food! Nude food is fresh fruit, wrapped in its own natural fruit skin. Think of bananas, oranges or apples, grown naturally in their own skins. Or maybe you use paper wrap to cover a sandwich or snacks. If you do, the waste will only take a couple of weeks or months to decompose back to nature.

On the other hand, if your lunch is wrapped in plastic, it will take much longer to break up. One packet of chips, a sandwich bag or a squeezable yogurt will add to the lunchbox lifetime. It only takes a few minutes to eat your lunch each day, but the impact of plastic packaging can last a lifetime. Choose wisely next time you reach for a snack or pack your lunch. You and your family are making important plastic-saving choices!

A collection of everyday items in lunchboxes. Which lunchbox is the eco-friendliest? What's inside? Is there plastic wrap? Paper? Or is it all nude food? Which lunchbox could you outlive?

◀

Longest lunch ever
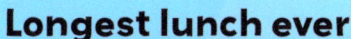

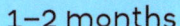

1–2 months   50 years   100+ years

Lunchbox lifespan

You will be at school for about 13 years – think about how many lunches you'll have during those years. If each and every lunch is packaged in plastic, then this will add up to one big plastic problem by the time you leave school! Can you go 'nude' with your lunch?

80 years   160 years   240 years

 Lifespan of a chip packet.

Plastic future thinking

Can you imagine 400 years into the future? It's hard, isn't it? Imagine who will see the plastic waste we are creating today. What will be left behind? Are we passing on waste to the next generation and generations beyond to deal with? What are our choices? How can we change our plastic waste story?

Natural waste footprints of the past

Today we can look back over tens of thousands of years of Indigenous culture to see the waste they created. One interesting place to discover waste is a **midden**, a place where Indigenous people ate together. Middens can tell a story about the foods that were eaten, the way they were prepared and shared.

Found all along the Australian coast, middens show how the waste that was created was natural. Most middens are made up of shells from shellfish and bones from fish or animals that were cooked and eaten. Middens show how Indigenous groups left only natural waste behind. What waste footprint do we leave on our Earth and in our oceans now?

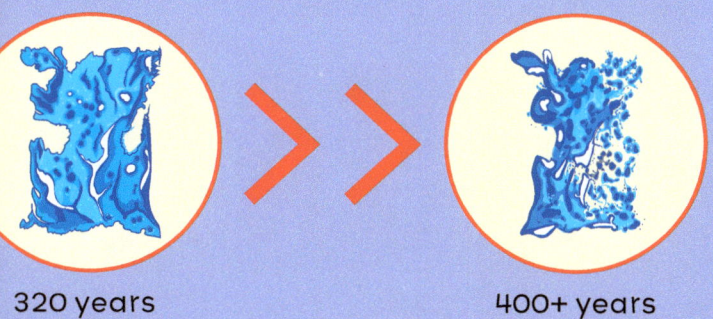

320 years >> 400+ years

Technology fossils of the current age

The plastic that is sitting in rubbish tips or drifting to the ocean floor may leave a lasting impression. Plastic bottles, bits of broken plastic, technology waste and plastic packaging could become the **technofossils** of the future. Could our plastic waste create a plastic imprint in future fossil records?

Chapter 5: A lifetime of plastic

Plastic ocean floors

The first ever global estimate of microplastics on the sea floor is just in! **CSIRO** scientists have calculated that over 14 million tonnes of microplastics have drifted down to the sea floor. That's more than double the amount of plastic estimated to be floating on the surface!

To make this discovery, deep sea robotic submarines investigated the sea floor. They were sent 3000 kilometres down, in a remote location 380 kilometres off the coast of South Australia. The underwater robots removed **samples** from the sea floor using a cylindrical core. Imagine a robot arm pushing a long round cylinder (like a cookie cutter) into the soft layers of the sea floor. The soft sea floor sediments made of silt were removed and brought back to the surface. The scientists then used high-powered microscopes and counted the number of microplastics found in each sample. Even the deep ocean is collecting our plastic waste! It is time for us to stop using single-use plastics to end this plastic pollution.

Chapter 6

IMPACTS ON OCEANIC WILDLIFE

Chapter 6: Impacts on oceanic wildlife

Plastic mimicry

In the ocean, looks can be deceiving. Sometimes things that look like food are not what they appear to be. Ocean-dwelling creatures use their **senses** to work out if food is safe to eat. Most marine creatures rely on sight or smell to help them find food.

Did you know that sharks can detect the electric pulse of their prey in the water? Or that oceanic seabirds can smell their feeding areas kilometres away in the open ocean? They use their super-sensitive **olfactory noses** and **nostrils** to smell krill swarms or bait balls in the surface waters of the ocean!

Have you ever noticed that a fish has nostrils? It helps them detect chemical signals of food or potential predators in the water. Fish can actually smell underwater, using the sensory pits in their olfactory nose. Fish use this clever feature to find food but can be tricked into eating plastic junk food if they are not careful!

Once marine creatures find food, they have to eat quickly before it escapes or disappears. Often creatures eat their prey before they've had time to properly inspect it. This is a problem if your food is not what you thought it was. Plastic, in all its many forms, can fool marine wildlife into thinking it is food, such as animals that are enticed by plastic bags that look like jellyfish.

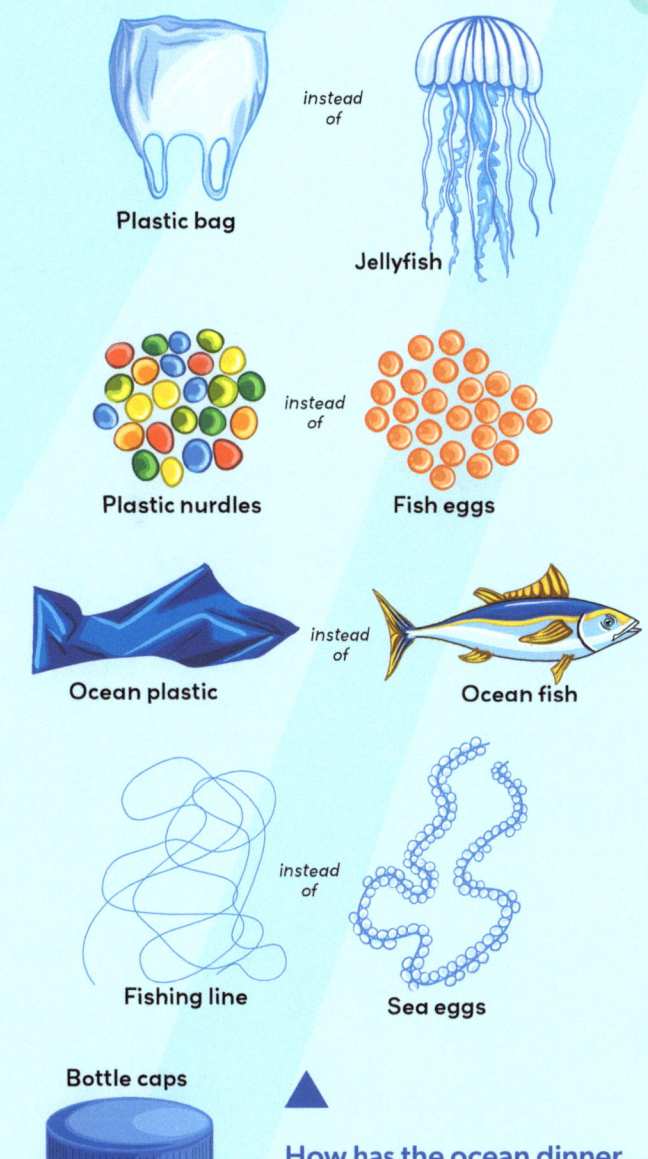

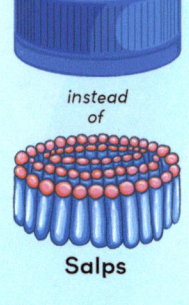

How has the ocean dinner menu changed? Plastic bags or jellyfish, plastic pieces or fish, bottle caps or **salps** are just the beginning for marine diners in the 21st century. What else could be served on the new menu of ocean food?

Krilling it – ocean plastics for dinner?

Why are anchovies eating plastic and not krill? Are they being tricked into eating plastic? Fish scientists set out to discover if anchovies are consuming plastic and why they might be doing this. Here are the facts they know:

- **Fact 1:** Anchovies are small fish that swim in schools.
- **Fact 2:** Anchovies love to eat krill and use their sense of smell to find them.
- **Fact 3:** Plastic emits a smell like food, which fools the anchovies into seeking it out and eating it.
- **Fact 4:** Marine predators, especially bigger fish, eat anchovies.
- **Fact 5:** Anchovies are an essential part of the marine food web.
- **Fact 6:** When anchovies eat plastic, everything in the **food chain** eats plastic.

When plastic items float at sea, after a few weeks bacteria and algae begin to grow as a thin layer or biofilm on the items. The **theory** is that bacteria covers the plastic and releases a smell in the water. Anchovies mistake this for the smell of food and then eat the plastic, thinking it was a meal of krill.

To test their theory, scientists made three solutions: 1) New clean plastic in seawater, 2) Old plastic pieces soaked in seawater, and 3) Krill soaked in seawater. The anchovies behaved as if there was food nearby when exposed to either the krill solution or the plastic pieces solution.

The anchovies' feeding behaviour confirmed the scientists' theory that the plastic pieces covered with a biofilm smelt similar to krill. A lot of plastic fragments were needed to release enough of the smell to mimic food. This is important because of the large concentrations of plastic found in ocean gyres.

Anchovies are vital to the survival of many fish species in the world and are also consumed by seabirds travelling across the ocean. Marine life and oceanic birds are smelling the bacteria and microbes that cover plastics in the ocean, mistaking them for food and eating plastic!

Chapter 6: Impacts on oceanic wildlife   59

Many ocean creatures such as sponges, clams, krill, baleen whales and feather stars are filter feeders. They filter their food out of the water and don't select it at all. These marine species catch whatever drifts past in the water, so even microplastic fibres can be taken in as a food source. Invisible plastic fibres are then stored inside their bodies!

Fish and other animals are eating plastics as part of an ocean food chain. Plankton absorb microplastics and are then eaten by small fish, small fish are eaten by bigger fish, big fish are eaten by humans, and all of a sudden plastic is carried up the food chain to us.

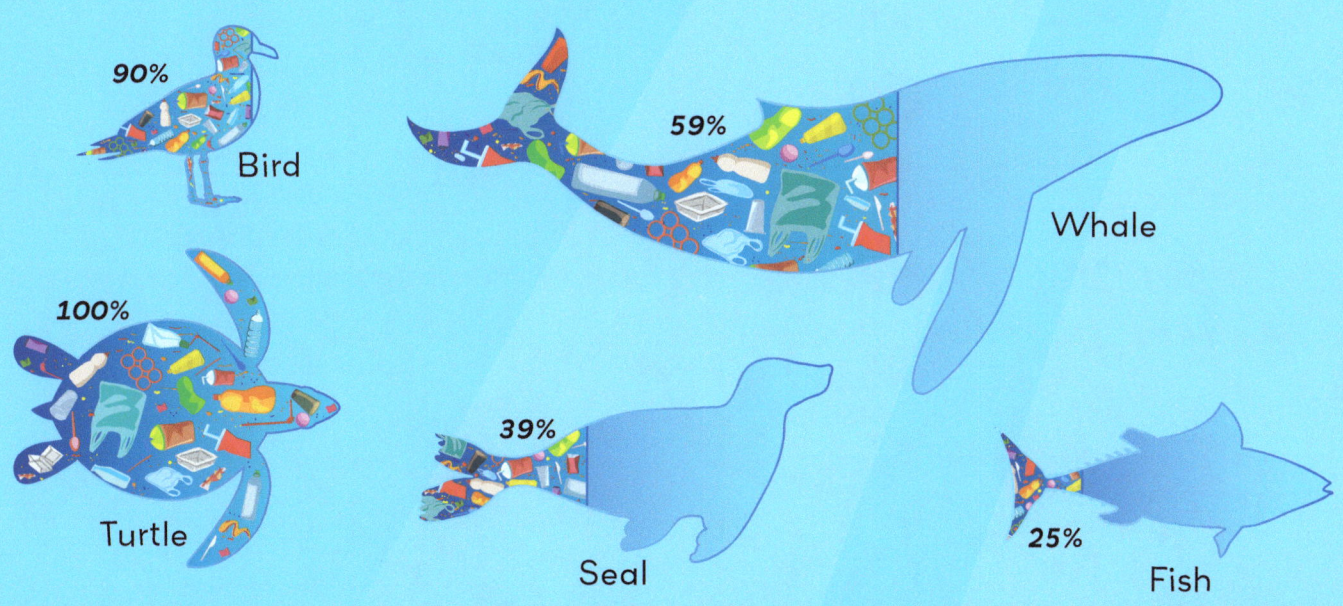

▲

Which species are most affected by eating plastic? All species of turtle (100 per cent), 90 per cent of bird species, 59 per cent of whale species, 39 per cent of seal species and 25 per cent of all fish species were found to have eaten plastic.

Oceans of Plastic

Food web connections

Energy passes along a food chain as animals eat or are eaten. An ocean food chain is made up of seaweeds, seagrasses, algae and marine creatures of all shapes and sizes. Every living thing in the ocean is part of a food web formed by connected food chains. These food webs form ocean ecosystems.

Let's dive in and discover how food webs work and how plastic gets into food webs.

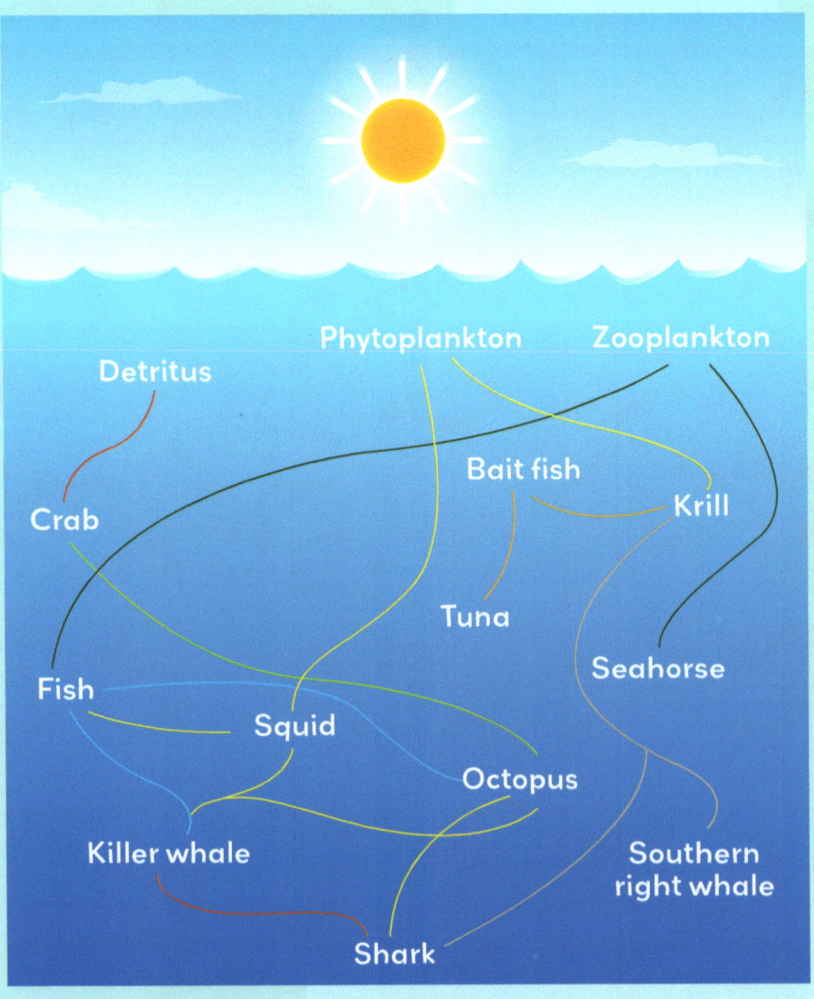

◀ Follow the feeding pathways to find the connections between living things in the ocean food web. Living things depend on each other for food. Food chains connect together, and create larger intricate food webs. If one species is removed it can affect the balance of the ocean food web.

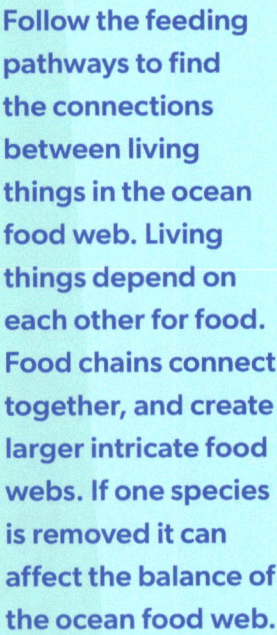

Chapter 6: Impacts on oceanic wildlife

Ocean food webs

Ocean food webs are powered by the sun's energy. Sunlight in the seawater is taken into the cells of tiny phytoplankton. In these cells, the sunlight powers the process of photosynthesis, where carbon dioxide and water are transformed into sugars helping the phytoplankton to grow. As they grow, they become an energy-packed food source for other living things to eat. Seaweeds and seagrasses also produce food by photosynthesis.

Some marine creatures eat only plants. These are the ocean herbivores. They can be massive creatures like dugongs that weigh 500 kilograms and eat 30–40 kilograms of seagrass per day. Or they can be the size and weight of a paperclip, like krill. Krill are one of the most abundant creatures in the ocean. As herbivores, krill eat phytoplankton and turn them into energy-packed protein. Swimming in massive swarms, krill are an essential power-packed food source. Ocean food webs depend on krill!

The food webs in the oceans are made up of different creature combinations. Krill are eaten by whales and ocean fish. Squid are eaten by dolphins and turtles. Sharks eat turtles, fish, seals, octopus and crabs. Energy is transferred from one living thing to the next.

Munching on marine plastic dinners

When marine creatures eat plastic for dinner instead of natural food it causes serious problems. The plastic takes up space in their stomach, reducing the amount of food they can eat. Then, the creature feels full even though they have not eaten enough. Some migratory species, such as birds, fish or whales, travel long distances and need to store energy for their journey. They need natural food, free from plastic pollution, if they are to survive.

Delicate digestion

The **digestive system** contains the stomach and intestines. These organs absorb the nutrients in food and expel waste. The food is turned into energy to fuel creatures to swim, fly, dive, mate, hunt and play. When animals eat plastic, it can cause blockages in the digestive system and stop the creature expelling waste such as poo or gas. Gas can build up in the body, causing bloating, which makes the creature float to the surface. This can make the animal vulnerable to attack, or take it away from its food source, so that it may be killed or starve.

It is difficult for animals to get rid of plastic once it is in their bodies. Often the piece of plastic is small enough to be eaten but too large to be digested and expelled. Ouch! The plastic can remain in the stomach for days, months or even years. Put simply, the more plastic a creature eats the bigger the problem becomes.

How does plastic enter the food chain? Plastic is finding its way into ocean food webs. How is it passed up the food chain? ▼

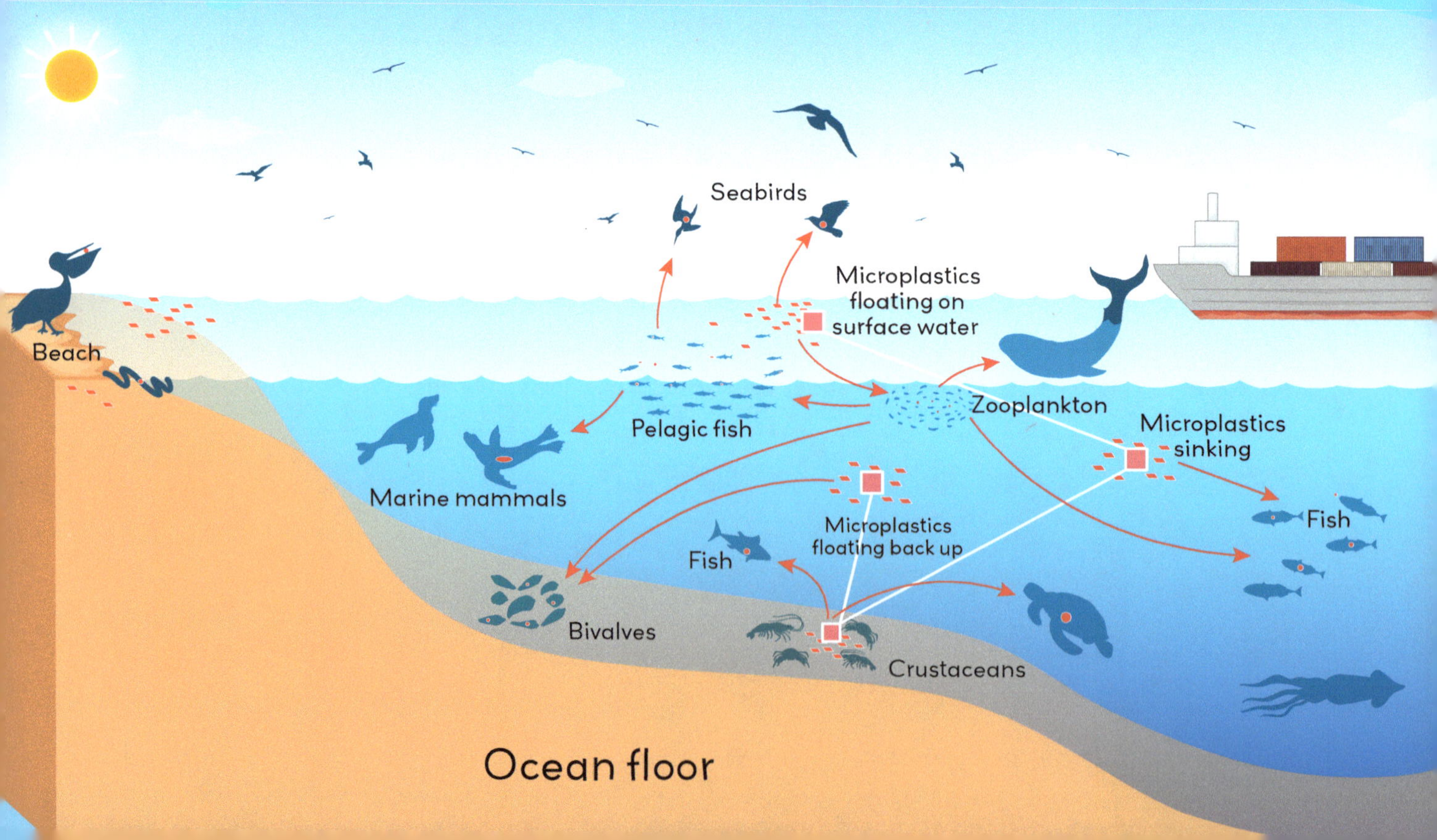

Chapter 6: Impacts on oceanic wildlife

See food and eat it!

Opportunistic feeders are not fussy eaters. They don't specialise in one kind of food, but eat a variety of different things. These creatures catch whatever passes by. Marine turtles are a great example of opportunistic feeders. Turtles eat different types of food such as green seaweeds, delicate sea anemones and jellyfish.

Floating plastic bags look a lot like jellyfish. If a turtle eats the plastic bag by mistake, it may cause a blockage. Gas can build up inside the turtle, making it float on the surface. As turtles dive down to catch their food, this is big problem!

Rescuing Tina

Tina, a green sea turtle (*Chelonia mydas*), was found floating in the Exmouth Gulf and brought into Bullara Station in Western Australia, then taken to the Ningaloo Sea Turtle Rehabilitation Centre at Exmouth. She had been floating on the surface long enough to allow barnacles to grow on her back. A team of people helped Tina. Dr Jane Giliam, the local vet who set up the Ningaloo Sea Turtle Rehabilitation Centre, ensured Tina had fresh food and a safe and comfortable tank to rest in. Then everyone waited for her to eat or to poo! This would show if Tina had eaten plastic and if her stomach was bloated. Or it may reveal that there was another explanation for why Tina was unwell.

Susie Bedford, a turtle rescue volunteer, found that Tina had been feeding on sea anemones, not plastics. She had just eaten a little too many of those squishy delights and Tina's gut had filled with gas, which made her float.

Volunteers at the rehabilitation centre have rescued over 19 sea turtles in the past 3 years, with 12 successfully released back into the ocean. Everyone is excited when the turtles recover and can be released back into the warm waters of the Ningaloo Reef.

Turtles around the world are not so lucky. Research tells us that over 52 per cent of the world's turtles have eaten plastics. The most common items are plastic bags, which turtles mistake for jellyfish. The plastic sits in their stomach, making them feel full. Turtles also get tangled in floating fishing nets. The nets can stop turtles surfacing to breathe so that they drown.

If turtles make it to their nesting grounds safely, plastic waste on the beach can make it hard for turtles to dig nests in the sand. This can be a big problem for those turtles that return to the same nesting beach on which they were hatched. Turtles do not simply find a new beach to breed on, but stop breeding. Marine turtles feel the full effects of ocean plastics during their lives.

SCOTT GRAY

▲

Tina the turtle at the Ningaloo Sea Turtle Rehabilitation Centre. Tina was rescued and cared for, then released into the ocean when she recovered.

Hunting from above

Seabirds can tell us a lot about the health of the oceans. Seabirds cover large areas of ocean in search of food, which means they can also provide information about plastic in the oceans.

Denise Hardesty is a scientist from CSIRO who investigates ocean plastics and the impact it has on marine life including seabirds. Denise and her research team have found that oceanic seabirds feed in areas with high concentrations of plastic. They estimate that 99 per cent of all oceanic seabirds will have plastic inside them by 2050.

Eating plastic causes problems for seabirds in the same way it does for other animals. If seabirds have stomachs full of plastic they might not store enough energy for long-distance flying. This can be bad news for migratory birds. Some bird species fly from one end of the Earth to the other two times a year to feed, breed and look after their young.

Creature Feature

Chapter 6: Impacts on oceanic wildlife

Short-tailed shearwaters and plastic oceanic journeys

▲ Short-tailed shearwaters out on the open ocean. The ocean is their home. Hunting and feeding over the waves of the ocean, shearwaters are tricked into eating plastic for dinner.

Short-tailed shearwaters (*Ardenna tenuirostris*) fly on migration journeys of over 30 000 kilometres around the Pacific Ocean each year. They fly from Bass Strait south of Australia to northern feeding grounds in the Bering Sea off Japan, Siberia and Alaska to feed in the Arctic summer.

These shearwaters live to 30 years of age and fly over 900 000 kilometres in their lifetime. That does not include local feeding flights when they are nesting. At the end of the nesting season, when raising their young, the short-tailed shearwaters fly up to 2000 kilometres to the icy seas off Antarctica to feed.

The shearwaters save energy by gliding – flying close to the water. Shearwaters are able to fly up to 600 kilometres in a day in long flights. This flying pattern remarkably helps them to save energy on their long journeys. The energy they get from squid and small fish like anchovies is vital for birds who must fly so far. Shearwaters have a keen sense of smell to help them find food, which they hunt for in the open ocean.

Shearwaters usually feed in the top layers of the ocean, from 1 to 5 metres down, but they can dive to 10 metres to chase swimming prey using their strong wings and webbed feet.

Not only does floating plastic smell like food, but pieces found floating near the surface layers can easily be mistaken for food. From above, plastic pieces may look like the flash of a fish or the glimmer of squid. A diving shearwater can collect lots of plastic items on its ocean journey.

Oceans of Plastic

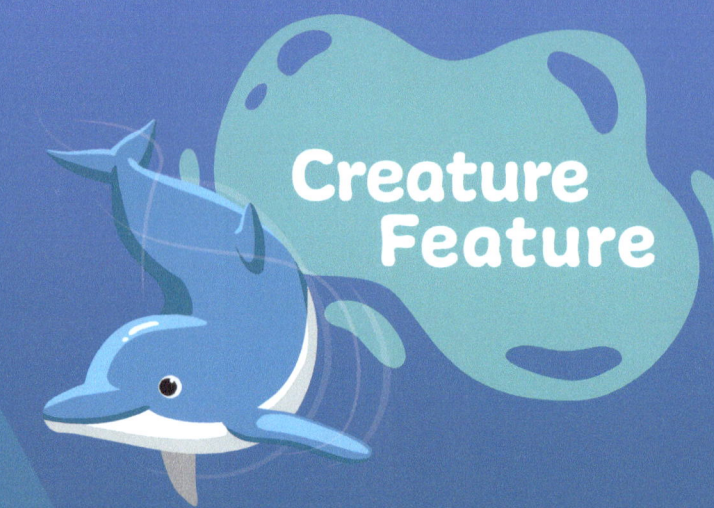

Creature Feature

Hooded plovers undercover

Nurdles look like fish eggs floating in the sea, but when they wash ashore, shorebirds can mistake them for food. Shorebirds like hooded plovers (*Thinornis rubricollis*) scurry along the beach searching in the wet seaweed for the sand hoppers (amphipods) that live there. Sand hoppers recycle seaweed into beach nutrients as well as feed shorebirds.

Sand hoppers are pale and round, and a similar size to nurdles. They usually spring off when disturbed. Hooded plovers snap up these energy-packed critters as quickly as they can before they hop away. If a hooded plover mistakes a nurdle for a sand hopper and eats it by mistake, it could get sick from the pollutants absorbed by the nurdle. It is also at risk of eating plastic rather than natural food sources. These threats are serious, so let's hope that the hooded plovers are too smart to eat nurdles.

DAN LEES

▲

Hooded plovers on the shore. Hooded plovers live their entire life on the shore – feeding, nesting and raising their young on ocean beaches.

Chapter 6: Impacts on oceanic wildlife   67

◀ Sand hoppers on the sand – a favourite food source of the hooded plover. They use their pale sandy colour as camouflage to blend into the beach habitat.

◀ Nurdles found in the sand. These small plastic pellets are a similar size and shape to sand hoppers – one of the natural food sources of hooded plovers.

◀ When nurdles are found among seaweed they blend in. Hopefully the hooded plover does not mistake the nurdle for a sand hopper.

Human connection

Feel like eating a credit card each week? Or having a teaspoon of plastic sprinkled on your cereal every Saturday? On average, we are eating 5 grams of microplastics each week. The plastic is hidden, eaten in food or slurped down from refilled water bottles. Invisible plastics are making their way up the food chain and into our stomachs.

Feeding on plastic POPs

Chemicals called **Persistent Organic Pollutants** (**POPs**) are found in the oceans. These chemicals are created to do many different things, such as kill pests (pesticides) or stop fires (fire retardants), but they are also produced by industries when they are making products. These **pollutants** are invisible in the ocean. If swallowed, POPs are easily stored in the flesh or tissues of living things. The POPs become part of their bodies and can be passed on along the food chain.

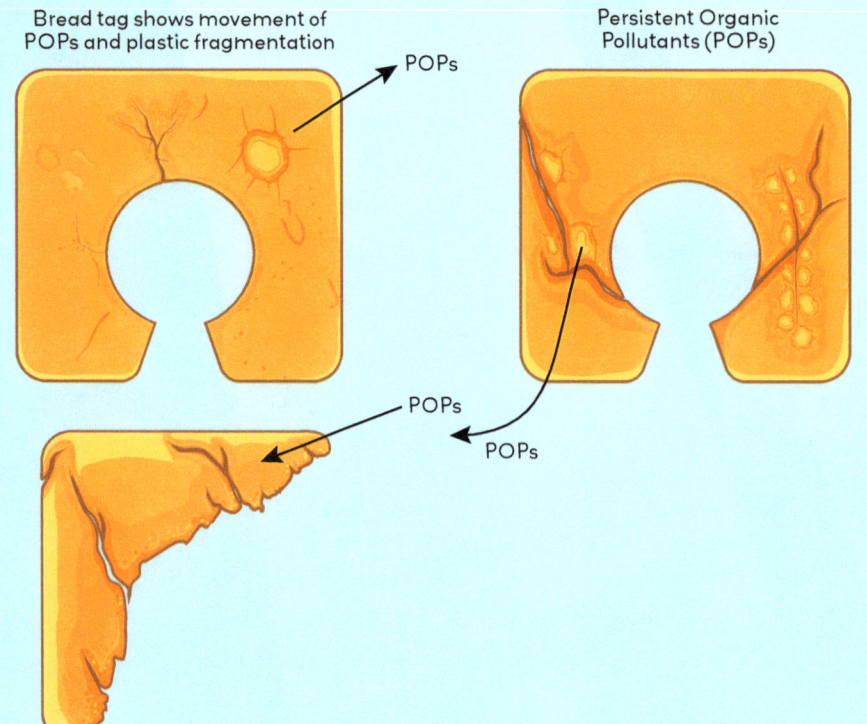

POPs in the plastic. Take the humble bread bag clip. It's made from a hard form of polystyrene, which floats and is easy to break. The plastic releases chemicals into the ocean and also soaks up chemicals.

Chapter 6: Impacts on oceanic wildlife   69

The organic pollutants are attracted to ocean plastics and attach to their surfaces, becoming more concentrated over time. For example, plastic nurdles can be coated in chemicals, but once in the sea they absorb POPs. Nurdles can hold one million times more POPs than the surrounding seawater. If the nurdles are eaten by a fish, those poisonous POPs become a problem for not only the fish that ate them, but all of the other fish, sharks or even us, that consume it.

Building up in the food chain

Each link in the food chain connects to the next. Part of the food that each creature consumes is stored in its body as muscle, fat and organs. When creatures eat microplastics, chemicals from the plastic enter their cells or tissues and the **toxins** from the plastic are stored in their bodies.

Everything is connected in an ocean food web. The plastic leaks chemicals into the water. The creatures use the water to filter their food or actively eat the plastic, resulting in the chemicals being stored in the body of the creature.

The higher up the food chain we go, the more plastic and poisons we find. Each link in the food chain collects the pollution from the creature before, so all the toxins in all the animals eaten are passed on to the bigger animal that eats them. The scientific term for this is **bioaccumulation**. We collect small amounts of plastics in our bodies as a top-order consumer, so this is something to consider when we choose our food. Plastic is a part of our food chains, affecting not only our ocean wildlife but all of us.

Marine life under threat

One in three species of marine mammals have been found entangled in marine litter. Over 700 marine animal species are believed to be threatened because of plastic pollution in the ocean. Marine life is affected by ocean plastics.

Chapter 7

MARINE SCIENCE IN ACTION

Marvellous marine scientists

Scientists work in different areas of science to learn about the ocean. Oceanographers study the open ocean and ocean floor. Marine biologists investigate life within the ocean. Marine ecologists are interested in how ocean habitats and ecosystems work. Ocean hydrologists study water movements. Some scientists such as marine toxicologists study how animals are affected by plastic, while marine chemists investigate the way that plastic and chemicals behave in seawater. They are all gathering information and trying to understand more about the health of the Earth's oceans and how plastic is affecting it. This is important, because the health of the world's oceans affects not only us but the health of global ecosystems. Scientists are working with people, communities, governments and businesses to help create solutions to the problem of plastic.

What questions are the scientists investigating? What can we learn from them? How is their work helping to find solutions?

Here are some of the questions scientists are asking:
- What impact does plastic have on marine life? And on people?
- How will plastic pollution affect the future of our oceans?
- How can science help solve the problems of plastic?

A record of ocean plastic

Over 60 years ago, a piece of plastic twine was caught in something called the **Continuous Plankton Recorder** or CPR. The CPR was used to study plankton, but scientists have gone back through its records to learn about ocean plastics. The plastic twine became the first sample of recorded marine plastic. Then the first plastic bag was caught in 1965, over 55 years ago! The survey is still going today, and it holds the longest continuous record of marine plastic samples ever undertaken.

Plastic research was big in the 1970s and 1980s, with marine scientists first warning people about the problem of plastic in our oceans and beaches. In the 1990s plastic research was bigger than ever with Captain Moore's

Oceans of Plastic

crossing of the Pacific Ocean. Since then scientists have studied microplastics and chemicals leaking from plastics and accumulating on plastics. As our knowledge grows, we understand that the problem is much bigger than we imagined.

Science in focus

Marine entanglement

Floating ropes, fishing nets and buoys form a large part of plastic pollution. These are lost or discarded by fishing vessels. The fishing industry uses specialised fishing equipment to catch different types of fish, shark, squid, crayfish and other seafood. Fish farmers grow marine species like salmon, oysters and mussels for people to eat. Unfortunately, sometimes animals that are not meant to be caught in fishing equipment become **entangled** and are killed or injured. Researchers found that 5.7 per cent of all fishing nets, 8.6 per cent of all fish traps and 29 per cent of all fishing lines are lost at sea, leaving a tangled trail in our oceans.

TRACEY GRAY

Watch out whales! Whales can become entangled with fishing gear of all shapes and sizes including fishing nets and craypot lines. As air-breathing mammals this can become a big problem very quickly.

Marine entanglement: helping out a southern right whale

Southern right whales (*Eubalaena australis*) move along the coast of Australia each winter. They migrate from the cold waters of Antarctica to give birth to their young. The female whales come close to the coast and beaches to give birth to their calves. This allows us to whale watch and see this amazing part of a whale's life cycle, but it does create risks for the whale. Whales and fishing industries use the same water. One of these industries harvests the southern rock lobster (*Jasus edwardsii*). So, how does fishing for lobster affect the whales?

Whales swim in deep water over rocky reefs where rock lobsters live. To catch lobsters, traps or pots are left in the ocean. These pots are attached to a buoy on the surface by a long line of rope. Buoys mark the spot where each lobster pot can be found underneath the water. If the whales swim over a lobster-pot line and their tail becomes entangled it can become a problem. Whales are at risk of being caught up in the rope lines that are attached to crayfish pots. The whale's tail can be caught, preventing it from diving or surfacing to breathe.

Over the years scientists have worked with the local fishing industry to help free whales that have become entangled. They now have a planned response to a whale being caught up and work together to help free the whale:

> *It's a wild day with a rough sea in south-west Victoria. People have spotted a whale that has become entangled in a lobster-pot line. They call the wildlife officers, who call the local marine entanglement group. Wildlife officers, whale watchers, scientists and the local fishermen spring into action. They meet at the boat ramp, with the marine entanglement gear. The boats are launched, and head out to sea through big waves. It's a very challenging task. The whale is stressed, the boats have to be positioned perfectly and everyone must know what to do. As they approach the whale, they use blades attached to long poles to cut the rope and free the whale. The whale flicks its tail and dives down, free.*

Ghost-net hunters

Ghost nets are discarded or lost fishing nets. They are held up by their floats, and capture all types of marine animals, making them a floating death trap. These fishing nets can be huge, and they can also wash onto the shores of some of the most beautiful beaches in the world.

One type of net, the **purse seine net**, is designed to catch a whole school of fish. The net can be 2000 metres long and reach down to a depth of 600 metres like a wall. Once the school of fish is encircled, the net is then pulled in at the bottom, closing it like a purse with the fish inside. The net is then brought onto the ship so the fish can be sorted and packed to be sent to market.

Purse seine nets capture a whole school of fish. The nets become a problem when they break away from their fishing boat or are discarded and float at seas as ghost nets. They trap and entangle marine creatures as they drift on ocean currents.

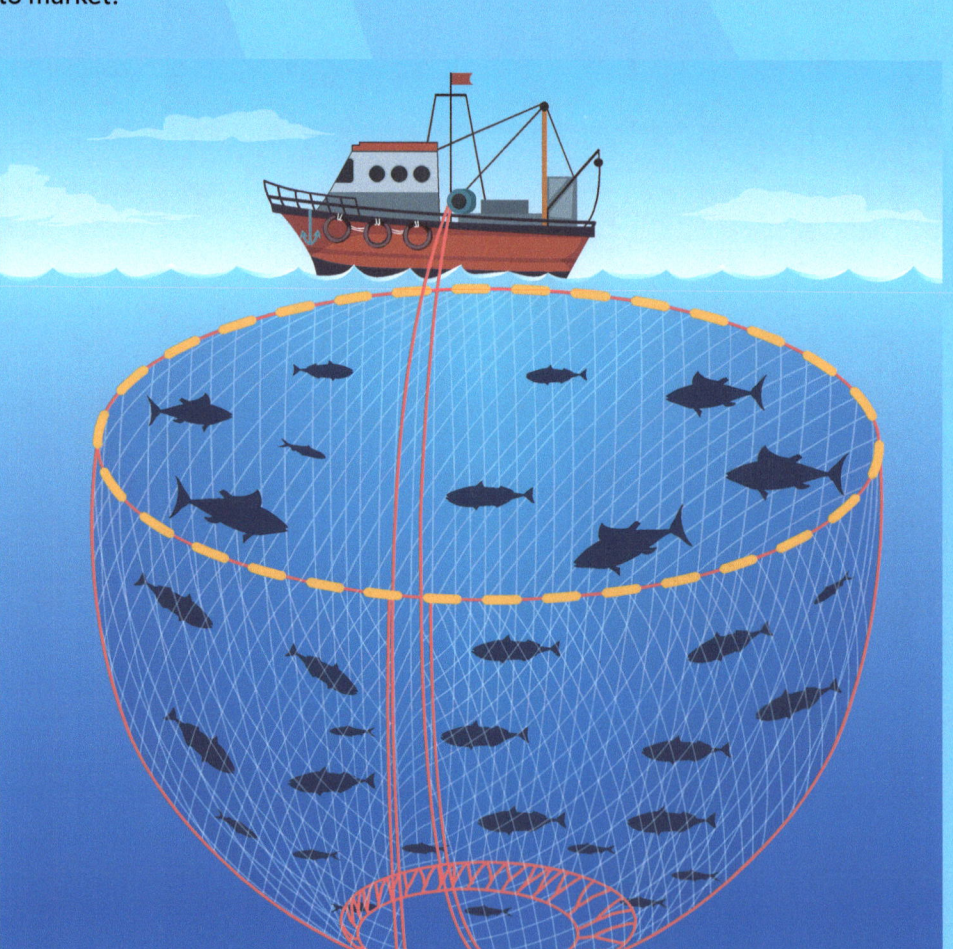

On the beaches of northern Australia ghost nets are washed ashore. Tangled on the shoreline, the nets are hard to remove. In the ocean the nets trap ocean creatures and become caught on boat propellers.

Important Indigenous rangers

A special science program is running in the Gulf of Carpentaria in Australia. The program involves 18 Indigenous communities with 90 Indigenous rangers working with scientists to find and remove the nets. The rangers scan remote beaches for ghost nets.

In the first few years they found 5532 ghost nets washed ashore. This number has tripled with over 15 000 nets found and removed. The ghost nets trapped over 15 000 marine turtles! What a sad story for the marine turtles that became tangled in the fishing gear.

Ocean wanderers

For scientists wishing to research ocean plastic, shearwaters are a good species to study. They return to their nests in burrows every night. In breeding season, they leave an information trail of what they have encountered during the day at sea when they return to feed their chicks.

Research scientists like Jennifer Lavers are not surprised to find plastic pieces in seabirds' stomachs. In one study of flesh-footed shearwaters (*Ardenna carneipes*) she found over 200 pieces of plastic in one seabird on Lord Howe Island. Her work includes flushing the plastic out of the birds' stomachs so they can eat and put on weight.

One of the most surprising findings was that almost all of the shearwater chicks had plastic pieces in their stomach. These chicks are not old enough to have left the nest, but their parents feed them plastic in their evening meal. This is a clear warning sign about the amount of plastics in our oceans.

Shearwater chicks like this one are being fed anchovies with a side order of plastic for dinner. Scientists work to remove the plastic out of the shearwaters' stomachs. They flush the plastic out with seawater, so the chicks can eat and grow into healthy adults.

Chapter 7: Marine science in action   77

Scientists have worked out that 8 per cent of a bird's bodyweight may be plastic. This is equal to a 62-kilogram person having 5 kilograms of plastic inside them! Or 12 pizzas' worth of plastic in your stomach. Can you imagine that? The plastic found in seabirds include parts of toothbrushes, bits of balloons and bottle tops.

The fulmar's lunchbox

The northern fulmar (*Fulmarus glacialis*) is the smaller cousin of the wandering albatross. They feed by skimming the ocean surface for food. Sadly, some of what they catch is plastic. This plastic addition to their diet is making them very unwell. Scientists have discovered on average 34 pieces of plastic are found in a northern fulmar stomach. If you scale that up to the size of a human that would be like having a full lunchbox-sized ball of plastic inside you! The plastic pieces are collected by the bird over several years. If they are lucky some plastic waste is pushed out of the body as bird droppings, otherwise the pieces stay inside the fulmar's body.

Seabird stomachs

Crunchy lunches! Ninety per cent of seabirds have some form of plastic in their stomach! Some chicks have eaten plastic before they even leave the nest. Scientists predict that by 2050 over 99 per cent of birds will have plastic in their bodies!

Oceans of Plastic

Creature Feature

Wandering albatross scour the oceans

Research scientists in the United Kingdom are investigating the largest seabird on the planet, the wandering albatross (*Diomedea exulans*). These ocean giants spend their life at sea, sometimes not touching land for a year. The albatross fly incredible distances over the oceans of the world, feeding in the surface waters. On remote islands they have found albatross nests made of plastics. In South Georgia these ocean giants are raising their young surrounded with plastic fragments.

DENISE HARDESTY

The plastic items mistaken for food eaten by this albatross are left behind. The plastic remains as the albatross's body decomposes.

Chapter 8

COMMUNITIES FOR CHANGE

Turning the tide on plastic pollution

We now understand the problem of plastics in our oceans. We can see the long-lasting impacts of plastic on marine life. Plastic is everywhere, and it cannot be ignored.

But we can start to change, and encourage each other to think and act for our oceans. We can pick up plastic rubbish when we see it. We can say no to single-use plastic items like straws, bags and packaging. Most importantly of all we can put plastic in the recycling bin. Everything we do counts, everything we do matters. Everyday actions have the power to create plastic-free oceans. The change is in our hands.

Bioplastics for the future

Bioplastics look like plastic and behave like plastic but are made of natural materials. If we can create a product that is made of naturally occurring plants or animals, then it will be quick and easy for microbes to devour. Scientists are working on ways to replace plastic products that we use every day.

Could juice from a prickly pear cactus replace petrol-based plastic? Scientists have made a chain of molecules that act like plastic but can be broken down in nature. The sticky juices of the cactus can be reformed into products similar to plastic items we use today but will break down in a matter of months.

Mushroom glue could be another new alternative to plastic products. Mushroom mycelium, the underground body of the mushroom, is made of long fibres. The mycelium is mixed with chopped up farm waste such as corn stalks, and then the mixture is pressed into a mould. The mushroom mycelium grows through the stalks, forming a strong shape. The items are then 'cooked' to stop the mushroom from continuing to grow. This mushroom glue could be used as an alternative to polystyrene packaging.

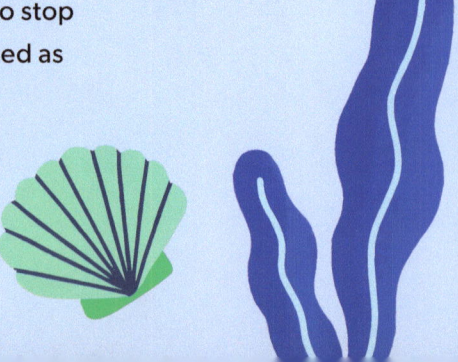

Lobsters and silkworms solving plastic problems

The shell or **exoskeleton** of a lobster is made of **chitin** (ky-tin). Chitin is a very common substance, found in crustaceans like lobsters, but also in insects and fungi. It is a protein that makes the lobster shell hard, flexible, water-resistant and strong, and yet it breaks down in nature leaving no trace. These are great properties for a lobster, and also great properties for plastic. When lobsters outgrow their shell, they peel off their old shell and the new shell underneath hardens when exposed to seawater. When new, lobster shells are soft and flexible. Researchers extract the chitin, powder it, add vinegar, process it and make a flexible plastic for bags, film, pots and other items.

A young school student, Angelina Arora, made headlines at the age of 16. She developed a bioplastic made from prawn shells and silkworms. After many trials she created a clear, flexible, strong material that acts like cling wrap. She discovered that by using sticky proteins of the silkworm (similar to those found in spider webs), the bioplastic was able to cling tightly to surfaces. The new natural material only takes 33 days to completely degrade. She was successful in developing a bioplastic that keeps food fresh and the planet healthy.

▲ Southern rock lobster (*Jasus edwardsii*) in the ocean. Rock lobsters and prawns have chitin in their exoskeletons. Innovative scientists are using chitin and silkworms to find new solutions to the ocean plastic problem. The lobster shells and silkworms completely break down and return to natural components without leaving a trace.

Fish guts smell yucky, but they can be used to produce oil. With some creative thinking and research this oil could be made into a bioplastic. It will take some time before these new plastic innovations hit the supermarkets, but scientists are continuing to research and develop new and exciting bioplastics for the future.

We need to be careful with the way we dispose of bioplastics as well. They need to be put into a healthy compost system full of hungry microbes to be composted. If they become litter they can break up like plastics, getting smaller and smaller, but will eventually decompose.

Take 3 for the Sea

Take 3 for the Sea is an award-winning environmental charity with a mission to reduce global plastic pollution. Take 3's simple call to action encourages people to 'Take 3' pieces of rubbish away before leaving a beach, waterway or anywhere. This action removes over 10 million pieces of rubbish from the environment every year. Take 3 has delivered education programs to 350 000 people around Australia. Take 3 aims to get more people to reduce waste and plastic pollution. It's amazing that 80 per cent of marine plastic pollution comes from the land. If we don't change our ways, by 2050 there will be more plastic by weight in the ocean than fish! By teaching small simple actions, Take 3 is helping everyone be part of the solution. Next time you're out in nature, Take 3 for the sea! It's all connected and it all helps!

DILLON MOUL

It's simple: Take 3 items of rubbish for a cleaner sea. This action can have a big impact. A small handful of rubbish removed from nature and put in a bin helps keep our oceans clean.

Tangaroa Blue Foundation and marine debris

Tangaroa Blue Foundation is a clever **citizen-scientist** program. The main aim of the foundation is to remove beach litter and work out what types of plastic are washing ashore. Volunteers collect the litter to clean up beaches and add information about it to the Australian Marine Debris Initiative (AMDI) Database. It is then shared with a large group of people working on where the plastics are coming from and how to get rid of **marine debris** and ocean plastics in the future.

Tangaroa Blue Foundation uses the term marine debris to describe any item made by people that ends up in our oceans or rivers. Plastics form a large part of the items floating in our environment. Tangaroa Blue Foundation and teams of volunteers clean up beaches and rivers, working along the foreshore to make a difference.

The clean-ups happen on a beach with volunteers walking for a set distance of at least 100 metres collecting all the rubbish that they find as they go. Once collected, the rubbish is sorted into waste groups. The groups include waste from fishing, household waste, medical waste, soft plastics and hard plastics. The information is added to the AMDI Database.

The AMDI Database helps to identify where each item of marine debris came from. The information can be used to track the waste back to the source. Here the information can be useful to report large rubbish spills or to see patterns of waste found on beaches or rivers.

Beach detectives

Have you ever wanted to be a detective working on a case, trying to solve a mystery? Well, collecting marine debris is a little like detective work on a beach. It is as simple as finding a plastic item and looking for the signs and symbols that can tell you where the item is from. We know that our oceans are all connected. Often the plastic you find is from your local area, but sometimes we find plastic items that have floated in from other countries around the world.

A plastic bottle found on the beach can tell an amazing story if you know what to look for. First, check if the bottle has a label. If so, you're in luck. It makes identifying the bottle easier. Check out the language it is written in. Can you read it or is it from a different country? Is the label a current design? Has the colour faded? Does it look like an old or new bottle? Some people have found bottles that are well over 50 years old on beaches.

Next, look at the lid. This is an essential part of the identification. What colour is it? Does it have any symbols imprinted in the plastic?

The next step is to find the source of the ocean plastics. What companies are responsible for the waste? Where was the waste found? What boat or ship may have lost the item? Tangaroa Blue Foundation works with companies that make plastic, helping these companies to be careful and responsible.

Citizen scientists in action

Tangaroa Blue Foundation is amazingly successful with over 150 000 people involved as citizen scientists assisting in the collection, sorting and data entry of ocean plastics. With the help of more than 1100 AMDI partners, they have removed over 15 million items from beaches and rivers and entered them as marine debris data. Tangaroa Blue Foundation and the beach clean-up volunteers and partners should be proud. The information is all at the fingertips of scientists and people caring for our oceans.

Message in a bottle

Imagine a beach full of thousands of plastic bottles washed ashore. On an ocean clean-up day that's exactly what Tangaroa Blue Foundation volunteers found in Queensland. A whole bay of bottles. The bottles were collected, and the data recorded.

The bottles looked new and hadn't been in the ocean for very long. Could the bottles have fallen off a boat? Or perhaps floated in on a local ocean current? It was interesting that the bottles were in good condition, but the label suggested that the bottles were from another country, with the writing in Vietnamese.

The team at Tangaroa Blue Foundation began investigating and with the help of government partners found the source of the bottles and the company was held responsible.

Where does our waste float away to? These plastic bottles washed ashore on a remote beach in northern Australia. The Tangaroa Blue Foundation discovered that the bottles had come from faraway places by checking the labels collected by beach clean-up volunteers.

Chapter 8: Communities for change

Communities in action

Pick up sticks

A beach littered in white plastic sticks – what are they from? Perhaps they were dropped from a ship carrying lollipops? Passionate beach walker and ocean conservationist Colleen Hughson first noticed the sticks on her daily beach walks in Warrnambool, Victoria.

Taking a closer look at the sticks Colleen noticed that not all the sticks were the same. Some had holes at the top and the others did not. What could they possibly be used for? They found out that the lollipop sticks had holes, and those without holes were the plastic stems from cotton buds.

Concerned with the number of cotton buds being washed up, Colleen created a call to action to 'pick up sticks'. Joined by local community volunteers and students, the team found and removed over 23 000 white plastic cotton-bud sticks off ocean beaches in the Warrnambool area.

How did these sticks end up in the ocean? Were people flushing them down the toilet? Or poking them down the drain? Did people know that they end up in the ocean, creating a plastic pollution problem that will not go away unless they are picked up?

The pick-up sticks message is to find 'better buds'. Switch to buying cotton buds with paper or **bamboo** sticks, not plastic, for the betterment of the ocean. Don't flush any cotton buds down the toilet or push them down the bathroom drain. Be careful how you dispose of waste. Talk to your friends and make a 'better buds' ocean pledge. Get active and pick up some plastic and help to bring an end to this preventable ocean plastic problem. Join the Better Buds campaign and switch your sticks for a plastic-free ocean.

Volunteers in Warrnambool, Victoria, including Elfie Bourger-Hughson, picked up an astonishing 23 000 plastic sticks from their local beaches. If only we switched to alternatives, like bamboo or paper.

COLLEEN HUGHSON

Chapter 8: Communities for change

Bubbles not balloons

Did you know that balloons can be dangerous for wildlife when they end up in the ocean? Balloons are one of the three most harmful floating items on the ocean surface. Scientists on Lord Howe Island are finding balloons and other plastic rubbish in over 80 per cent of seabird chicks that haven't even left their nest. Seabird parents have found the rubbish and delivered it for dinner.

So why are there so many balloons in the oceans? People use or release balloons at events, to celebrate or just for fun. If balloons are used outdoors they can float way up into the atmosphere before bursting and falling to Earth. On a planet that is 70 per cent water, they will most likely fall into the ocean.

Blow bubbles instead of balloons outdoors, especially at outdoor events where balloons can break free and blow away, out over the ocean. Balloons, strings and clips can end up in rivers, streams and drains where they are carried to the ocean. Simply switching from balloons to bubbles makes a massive difference for seabirds and marine life in our oceans, and who doesn't love bubbles?

ZOOS VICTORIA

Inspired to help seabirds, Zoos Victoria started a campaign to encourage people to run seabird-friendly events by changing how we use balloons or not using them at all and blowing bubbles instead.

4Ocean bracelets for change

The Galapagos Islands are remote and isolated, but plastic still washes up on their shores. The plastic affects the islands' incredible wildlife, such as the Galapagos sealions.

4Ocean is a business that removes garbage and rubbish from the oceans of the world and turns some of it into bracelets. For every bracelet purchased, 4Ocean promises to remove half a kilogram of waste. The sale of the bracelets helps funds waste removal. The bracelets are made from 100 per cent recycled plastic bottles, melted and turned into recycled thread. The glass beads are made from recycled glass as well. The bracelets close the recycling loop and are part of the solution to cleaner and greener oceans.

4Ocean run vessels specially designed to collect floating plastic waste from rivers around the world. This stops the plastic from reaching the sea. The plastic recovered from the water is sorted into colours, bundled and sent to recyclers to make new products.

4Ocean removed nearly 4.3 million kilograms of waste from the water in three years. They work in Haiti, Bali (Indonesia), Florida (America) and

TANGAROA BLUE FOUNDATION

Ocean plastics are in your hands. Everyday items like straws, balloons, take-away cups, twine, plastic bottles, caps and toothbrushes are washing up on the shores around the planet. Beach clean-ups happen worldwide. In Australia information from beach clean-ups can be recorded on a marine plastic debris database.

Guatemala (South America). 4Ocean is glad to have access to some of the most polluted rivers and oceans on the planet, employing local people to remove plastics from the water.

4Ocean involves people in many ways. It allows people around the world to contribute to ocean clean-ups by wearing a bracelet that is 100 per cent recycled. It has encouraged people to start conversations about our oceans and the plastics. These can be powerful ways to create change.

The Great Nurdle Hunt

The Great Nurdle Hunt is on. People from around the world are looking for nurdles on beaches and riverbanks. The Great Nurdle Hunt is a project of Fidra, a Scottish organisation that wants to rid the sea of nurdles forever.

We know that nurdles are not only coated in chemicals, they also absorb more chemicals once they enter the ocean. You can hunt for nurdles anytime, anywhere and record your finds on the Fidra website. Fidra encourages people to be citizen scientists and collect information to help solve the world's nurdle problem.

Creature Feature

Bottle flipping sealions in the Galapagos

The most abundant marine mammal on the Galapagos Islands is the Galapagos sealion (*Zalophus wollebaeki*). It is **endemic**, being found nowhere else in the world. The thousands of sealions are at home sunbaking on beaches, catching food and playing in the waters of the islands. Sealions have been spotted with something new. They have been flipping plastic bottles, playing with them like toys. The floating plastic bottle has sparked the seals' natural curiosity. The action of the seal flipping the bottle can speed up the time it takes to break up into smaller pieces! It is clear that plastic is not only reaching the shores of the Galapagos Islands, but can become a problem for wildlife. The impact of our plastic reaches far and wide, but we can be part of the solution, helping organisations to remove the plastic waste in faraway places of the oceans.

Each year a worldwide event is held in March. When the Great Nurdle Hunt is on, nurdlers from around the globe head to beaches to hunt for nurdles. The nurdles are collected and counted and added to the nurdle hunt database. The Great Nurdle Hunt becomes a snapshot in time of the number of nurdles in the environment. The data can be used as evidence when information is needed about nurdles as a form of plastic pollution.

Nurdles sometimes reach a beach in astonishing numbers, covering the beach like snow. Then it's all hands on deck to collect them (with caution and hand-washing after), count them and share the knowledge. This is important work for citizen scientists around the world who keep watch and help marine wildlife.

Organisations and communities have come together to make a change. They've inspired everyday actions that will help clean the ocean. From buying a bracelet and picking up plastic on the beach, to choosing to refuse plastic and recycling wisely, each of us has a way to help our oceans. We can be the change-makers of the future.

COLLEEN HUGHSON

▲
Nurdlers unite to make a clean sweep of our beaches in the Great Nurdle Hunt. Nurdles are tricky to find and hard to remove, but that doesn't deter the Nurdlers of the world from picking up microplastic one piece at a time.

Islands overrun with plastics

Have you ever seen 997 000 shoes? Or maybe 373 000 toothbrushes on the beach? If you go to Cocos Islands in the Pacific Ocean chances are you will see more ocean waste than you expected. Over 262 tonnes of plastic rubbish has washed ashore on the Cocos Islands. Scientists and volunteers count plastics while they clean up in an effort to help understand and find waste solutions for these islands far, far away.

Chapter 9

IDEAS, INSPIRATIONS AND INNOVATORS

Ideas are powerful

An idea can change so much. Tackling our biggest ocean plastic problems will take a lot of new ideas, inspirations and innovations.

There is no age limit on ideas. Some of the most inspirational change-makers are young people. Starting with a simple idea, they worked to make it a reality.

All brilliant ideas need work, time and people power to make them happen. Innovation starts with a bright idea, and a willingness to give the idea a go. A whole lot of trying, trialling, failing, rethinking and trying again is needed to innovate. Innovation is an essential part of stopping plastic pollution in our oceans.

Let's see some of the exciting ways people are tackling some of our biggest plastic-pollution problems.

StrawNoMore

Let's talk about straws. Most drinking straws are plastic, used once for a few minutes and then thrown away. Some people even put two straws in a drink. Over 10 million straws are used in Australia every day. In one year, that's a massive 3.5 billion straws thrown away! They end up everywhere, at the beach, in parks, in streets, in rivers and eventually in the sea.

StrawNoMore was started in 2017 by Molly Steer, an Australian girl who was 11 years old. She began the campaign after watching a documentary called *A Plastic Ocean*. She wanted to do something about plastic pollution.

Molly began the StrawNoMore program at her local school in her hometown of Cairns in Queensland. She talked to her school and encouraged her school principal to take action and remove the plastic straws from the school canteen. Her actions encouraged others. Students in other schools were inspired by Molly and became StrawNoMore schools. She wanted every school in tropical north Queensland to stop using straws. Being so close to the Great Barrier Reef, north Queensland was a fantastic place to start.

Chapter 9: Ideas, inspirations and innovators 93

Molly inspired local councils to make a change and ban straws from their region. She now has 'StrawBassadors' working around Australia to help rid the country of single-use straws. Molly has been on ABC Television's *War on Waste* series. Molly even has her own TED talk.

The StrawNoMore campaign asks people to take a pledge to stop using straws. It asks us to talk about the impact that straws have on our planet's oceans. Say 'no thanks' to straws and explain why when you are next offered one. You may change a shopkeeper's mind.

Working with nature to clean up the oceans

Seabins cleaning up one marina at a time

While travelling the ocean in search of great waves, two surfers saw oceans littered with plastic pollution. They came up with a brilliant idea: to create a bin that removed pollution from the ocean. They focused the litter-removing project on harbours and boat marinas. These areas are where rubbish often enters the ocean from boats, jetties and street runoff. The team spent their life savings to build the working **prototype** model.

The result was a floating Seabin that collects rubbish just like pool filters do, bobbing up and down in the water. The plastic waste drifts into the slow-moving backwaters of the harbour, just like the rubbish in ocean gyres, where it is sucked up by a carefully placed Seabin.

Seabins are innovative because they remove ocean plastics 24 hours a day. The filters can be taken out,

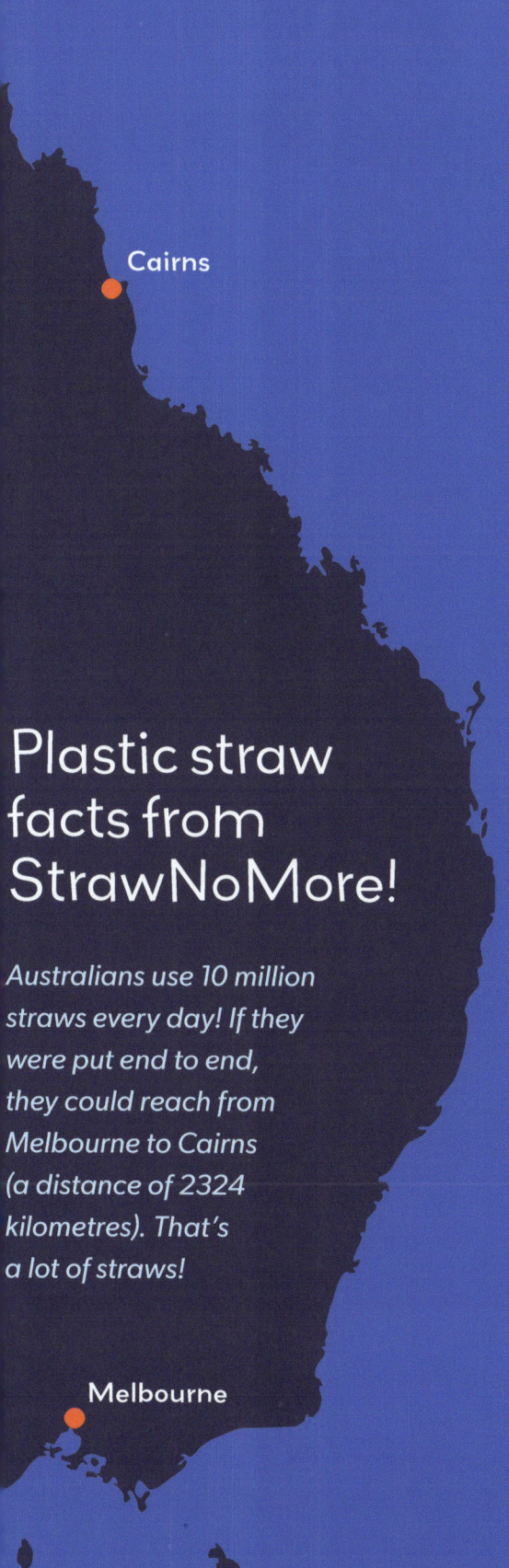

Plastic straw facts from StrawNoMore!

Australians use 10 million straws every day! If they were put end to end, they could reach from Melbourne to Cairns (a distance of 2324 kilometres). That's a lot of straws!

cleaned and replaced. The Seabins collect rubbish such as pieces of plastics, bottles, plastic packaging, fishing line and cigarette butts. The Seabin can also collect oil from the water. As there are lots of boats in a marina that leak or spill fuel, this is a bonus. The oils float on the top of the water and can be skimmed off into the Seabin and removed from the ocean.

The latest Seabin model brings more innovations. The fabric used in the mesh bag can remove microfibres from the water. The smaller mesh size allows the Seabin to remove microscopic threads. These microplastics or nanoplastics are harmful because they end up in the ocean and are eaten instead of food.

The Ocean Cleanup

The Ocean Cleanup is tackling the problem of ocean plastic on a massive oceanic scale. The ambitious task of this organisation is to remove 50 per cent of the plastic from the Great Pacific Garbage Patch every five years. The Great Pacific Garbage Patch is found in two locations between the coast of America and Japan, in the Pacific Ocean. The east garbage patch floats near Japan. In the west, the garbage patch floats between Hawaii and California.

Boyan Slat created The Ocean Cleanup. He was studying aerospace engineering but was inspired to work on ocean plastics when he was snorkelling in Greece as a 17-year-old. Seeing so much plastic in the water, Boyan wanted to make a difference. His plan was to remove plastic from the ocean's biggest garbage patches. He knew the task was enormous, but he wanted to try to solve the problem.

The team created an ocean collecting device to remove ocean plastics from the water. The collected waste is to be recycled and used to make new plastic items to fund future ocean clean-up programs.

The Ocean Cleanup program is a great STEM (Science, Technology, Engineering and Maths) project in action on a mission to solve this ocean-sized problem. The floating system makes use of the natural forces of winds, waves and currents to collect plastic in a giant floating rope loop. The rope loop is fitted with a net-like skirt that also collects underwater plastic fragments.

Chapter 9: Ideas, inspirations and innovators   95

The system works by drifting with the plastic. When the plastic pollution is concentrated inside the loop, it can be extracted by a ship. The Ocean Cleanup team conducted tests and trials to see how the plan works out at sea. With each test, new information was discovered, and the design was adjusted to solve the problems found.

The Ocean Cleanup team has recently created solar-powered boats called Inceptors to clean up rivers. The Inceptor is completely solar powered and does not require any human input to work. It collects floating litter to stop it reaching the ocean. The waste is caught on a boom arm coming out from the boat, then picked up on a conveyor belt and separated in the boat. The waste is then collected from the boat and taken for recycling. The Ocean Cleanup group has four vessels in the water, and they are working away at cleaning up the most polluted rivers on the planet.

Creature Feature

Discovering dolphinfish hideouts

Dolphinfish, or mahi-mahi (*Coryphaena hippurus*), live in warm open oceans; they are a **pelagic** fish and are designed to swim long distances. Dolphinfish live and feed near floating objects, using natural items like seaweed and coconut palm fronds as habitat. As plastic pollution fills our oceans, plastic is quickly becoming a common form of shelter in the open ocean. Hiding under plastic containers, or floating with drift nets, dolphinfish use them as temporary floating homes.

Dolphinfish make the most of the food that is available, often feeding in a frenzy. They definitely 'eat before they think'. This is a risky feeding strategy! People fishing for dolphinfish find plastic items in the gut of these ocean travellers, including bottle lids, cigarette lighters, rope pieces and parts of plastic containers. Dolphinfish remind us that we need to remove plastic from our oceans. It is up to us to refuse plastic, recycle plastic and always pick up plastics before they make it to the ocean.

Catching our waste

Have you ever thought about the litter that washes down the drain in the street? Where does it go? Is it heading to the sea? Or a wetland? Is the drain connected to a local river or stream? Where does that river lead to, and what happens to the litter that travels down the drain? How do we stop it from getting out to the ocean?

Litter traps could be the answer. Putting up a screen to catch the litter is one way that we can reduce waste reaching the ocean. Local governments all over the world are installing litter traps to help stop the flow of plastics into oceans.

There are lots of different designs for litter traps. Some float, some are permanent concrete structures, some use screens, but the newest idea is to use nets to catch the litter. The trash net bags expand when they are full of rubbish and are then removed, sometimes with the help of a crane. The waste can be sorted and taken to rubbish tips or recycling centres. The netting bag is then reset, ready to catch the next load of rubbish from the stormwater drains. If you know a local waterway with a whole lot of plastic, let your local council know. Ask what is being done to stop the litter in the waterway.

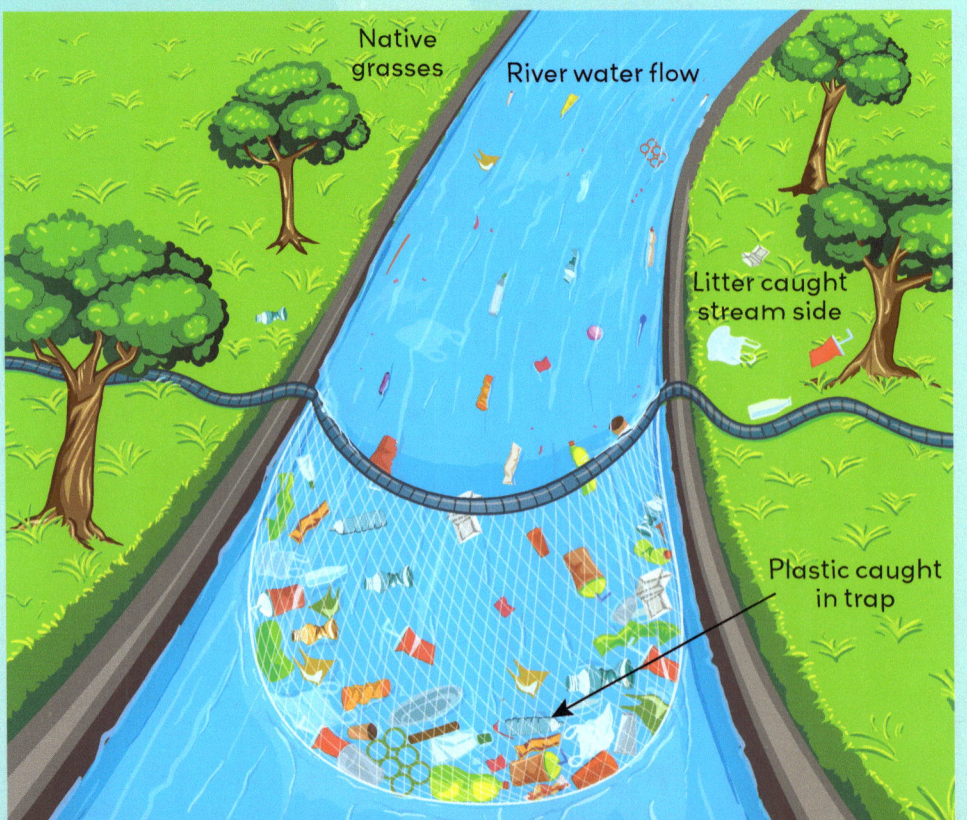

◀ Trap it in the street! These traps capture waste that is dropped in the street or blows down the road and into a local waterway. It is estimated that 90 per cent of the world's rubbish enters our oceans from only 10 main rivers of garbage flowing into the ocean.

Chapter 9: Ideas, inspirations and innovators

Plastic bags around the world

Over 5 trillion single-use plastic bags are being used every year, which adds up to a mind-blowing 160 000 bags per second! That's enough to cover a country the size of France in plastic bags – or, if you laid the plastic bags end to end, they would loop around the world seven times every hour! Large supermarket chains are now asking us to bring our own reusable bags. It's a small act, with a big impact.

Change is in the bag

Local communities are making big changes to the way they shop, especially in Anglesea and Port Fairy, at either end of the Great Ocean Road in Victoria. Being so close to the ocean comes with environmental responsibilities. Knowing the impact of single-use plastic bags on ocean wildlife, the two towns were inspired to act. In 2004, Anglesea became one of the first towns in Australia to eliminate plastic bags at the supermarket checkout and the town is now plastic-bag free.

Local schools in Port Fairy joined forces to encourage the town to go plastic bag free in 2008. Led by students and supported by families, the whole community wanted to see change.

The students asked local businesses to stop handing out single-use plastic bags. They asked shoppers to change their single-use bags for natural **cloth** bags. The See Change Bag Project sold over 2000 bags in the first few years of the program. The children created eye-catching marine designs. The successful designs were printed onto bags, which were sold at the local supermarket. They were a hit. The program was relaunched in 2016, a second design was completed, and the bags were back in stock.

This changed the way the town shopped, and people started switching to cloth bags – a big step for a small rural township of 3000 people. The program was sustainable, and it helped raise funds for local schools, with sales from the bag going to new sustainability projects at each of the schools.

TRACEY GRAY

Students can change the way plastic bags are used in their community. Port Fairy students created 'See Change Bags' in reusable material with appealing designs. To see the change, they had to be the change, inspiring others and creating waves of community change in their local area.

Inspiring leaders of the future

Have you ever seen a soy sauce sushi fish? They are single-use, soy sauce containers in the shape of a fish, often given out with sushi. If a year 6 primary student from Victoria succeeds, they may become extinct. Scarlett Rosshandler has collected over 73 000 signatures for her campaign. She wants to ban the single-use plastic fish. Help Scarlett's ocean crusade by saying no to the soy sauce sushi fish as well!

Did you know that Australia has its own plastic-free superhero! Arlian Ecker, is the 'Plastic Free Boy' of Byron Bay. He's on a mission to rid the world of plastic bags. Arlian is not shy in talking about the ocean impacts of plastic on turtles. He is happy to stand out the front of supermarkets to explain where plastic bags can end up or give speeches to sustainability leaders from around the world. He made a film 'Plastic Alarm' about the turtles to share the ocean plastic story. He wants to create change.

There are many stories of young ocean guardians around the world, showing that kids are not afraid to lead the way in stopping ocean plastics in their communities. They are true ocean activists!

If oceans could talk, what would they say?

Would oceans ask us to think about our rubbish that floats in its waves? Would they ask us to consider the creatures that need to feed, without eating plastic junk? Would they ask us to change our ways? I wonder, what would they say? We all need to find ways to change the plastic future of our oceans today.

Chapter 10

ACTION FOR THE OCEANS

Small changes for healthy oceans

Small changes can make a big difference. Every day we make choices that affect our world. Often, we feel as if our choices don't matter, but you have the power to make changes that will last a lifetime.

Be a change-maker. Find an ocean plastic program that matters to you. Whether you're passionate about marine creatures, interested in beach clean-ups or simply saying no to straws, your actions will make a difference.

Plastic footprints in the sand

Have you ever heard of a **plastic footprint**? A plastic footprint is a measure of the amount of plastic that you create each day, month or year. The measurement is important because it helps you understand the amount of plastic you use in your life. If we are to break our plastic habits, we need to find out what we are using so we can make better plastic-free choices.

The more plastic you use, the bigger your plastic footprint. If you use less plastic, your plastic footprint will be smaller. Find yourself some recycled paper and think about your day. Break it into morning, afternoon and evening. Let's look at some ways you can reduce your plastic footprint.

How big is your plastic footprint? Think about all of the plastic that you come into contact with in one day. This is a part of your plastic footprint. You can shrink your plastic footprint by choosing plastic-free products and finding plastic-free solutions.

Chapter 10: Action for the oceans   101

Prepare to break up with plastics

Breaking up with plastic can be hard. You have to be prepared and be smart. A great way is to prepare a bag to take when you are on the go. Think about where you're going and what you're doing. Use some of these ideas to help you on your plastic-free quest.

School day

Here are some ways to help our planet and avoid plastic waste:
- bamboo toothbrush
- shampoo bars instead of shampoo in bottles
- soap bars instead of body wash
- deodorant bars instead of deodorant in plastic bottles
- cotton buds with bamboo or paper sticks instead of plastic
- breakfast at home in bowls with spoons
- rubbish-free lunchbox packed with nude food (unwrapped of course)
- refillable drink bottle.

Sports activities

Get ready for action and adventure with a little kit of plastic-free goodness:
- refillable drink bottle or cup for hot drinks
- reusable snack pack filled with fruit and snacks (no single-use packs)
- fresh fruit as nude food to give energy on the go
- cloth towel for wiping hands and cleaning up before you eat.

Weekends – hanging out with friends

Be the leader of the pack when it comes to plastic awareness. Lead with kindness and offer solutions to your friends who might not have found the plastic-free path:

- refillable drink bottle or cup for hot drinks
- metal or bamboo straw, or insist on paper straws
- reusable snack pack (with fruit and snacks)
- eating in at cafes or restaurants to reduce take-away waste
- at the movies bring out your refillable cup and straws.

When your day is over, don't forget to unpack your rubbish-free pack. The cups, drink bottles, containers and straws will need to be cleaned. Take them out and wash them with hot soapy water. Dry and put them back into the pack, ready for your next plastic-free day.

Everyday examples of plastic-free packs to get you out and about on eco-adventures. Get inspired, get excited and get packing. You'll be on your way to a plastic-free day.

Eco-adventures

- School bag
- Lunch box
- Nude food
- Drink bottle
- Refill cup
- Refill drink
- Metal straw
- Towel
- Bamboo toothbrush
- Shampoo bar
- Bamboo straw
- Reusable containers
- Nude food packs
- Nude food packs
- Reusable bag
- Travel bag

Where is the plastic hiding out?

Become a plastic detective in your home. Find out where the plastic is hiding out. This is a simple idea that lets you discover where your family is using plastic products. Grab a pencil, some paper and get cracking. Create a mini plastic audit sheet to find out where plastic is hiding in your home.

Once the plastic is found, make some notes about each item. What type of plastic is it? Think up some ways in which you can change plastic for a different biodegradable or recyclable material.

In the kitchen

Kitchens are a favourite place for single-use plastics. Check the fridge, cupboards, pantry and under the sink for plastics. We need containers for food, but we can be wise and choose products in glass packaging or cardboard. If we must use plastic, we can wash it out and recycle it. If we have soft plastics, such as plastic bags or packaging, collect them and return them to a supermarket to be recycled.

When storing leftovers, use a bowl with a plate on top for a lid, or some of the silicone or waxed cloth wraps available, instead of cling wrap. Glass jars are also useful for leftovers.

In the bathroom

Plastics can accumulate and multiply in bathrooms. Check out the drawers under the basin as well as the bathroom cabinets. Bathroom plastics are stronger and need to be recycled. With a quick clean, containers can be recycled and go on to a new life as another plastic product. Switch to using shampoo bars instead of shampoo in bottles, and traditional soap bars instead of body wash. Bamboo toothbrushes can replace plastic toothbrushes and toothpaste tablets can replace plastic toothpaste tubes.

In the laundry

Check the cupboards and under the sink for washing liquids and cleaning products. These products come in many different types of plastic containers with spray nozzles attached. There are lots of great products for sale that help reduce laundry packaging. Think about using laundry detergent paper strips, which are designed to dissolve in the wash, and natural cleaners that can be refilled into reusable spray bottles. Microfibre capture balls can be added to your washing machine; they catch the microfibres from your clothes so that they don't get washed down the drain.

Creature Feature

Quit plastic and help a hermit crab

Hermit crabs (*Coenobita perlatus*) are the ultimate beach cleaners, scouring the beach looking for dead organic pieces of food to eat. Hermit crabs work hard to find food, and as a result keep beaches clean and healthy. Don't be fooled by their 'hermit' name – they may live alone in their protective shell, but they are part of a hermit crab community.

Did you know that hermit crabs use their sense of smell when looking to up-size their shells? They are attracted to the smell of dried out sea snails. They then try the sea snail shell on for size and if it fits, they move in.

As the crabs move along beaches, they find lots of single-use plastic items on the shore, which can become a dangerous trap. Once a hermit crab goes inside a plastic container, they can become stuck inside.

During the day plastics on beaches heat up, becoming too hot for the crabs to survive! The dead crabs release a smell similar to dead sea snails, attracting more hermit crabs. The plastic container has now become a lethal trap!

On the remote Henderson Islands, scientists found 526 dead hermit crabs in a single plastic container! It's time to quit plastic to protect our oceans, beaches and living creatures.

Chapter 10: Action for the oceans

Plastic switch out

Using items made from different materials is a great way to get plastic out of your life. What are some of the great choices available?

Bamboo is a great choice. It grows fast, locks in carbon as it grows, is reusable and can be used more than once before it heads to the compost bin.

PIPPILONGSTOCKING/SHUTTERSTOCK.COM

Metal is good; and it can be washed and reused. It does take a lot of energy to create metal items, not to mention digging minerals out of the ground and transporting them. Choose metal items carefully, use them wisely and care for them so they last.

OLGA MILTSOVA/SHUTTERSTOCK.COM

Cloth is an excellent choice, if it is from plants like cotton. Although cotton takes a lot of water to grow, it has a long lifespan and can be used over and over again. The impacts of its production are reduced the more times you reuse the bag. Cotton shopping bags or cotton dishcloths are great for everyday use. Beeswax wraps are a fantastic natural alternative to plastic wraps. A beeswax wrap is cotton fabric painted with beeswax to make flexible wraps that can keep your snacks fresh without plastic.

YESPHOTOGRAPHERS/SHUTTERSTOCK.COM

Remember these plastic-swapping ideas:

- Single-use plastic bottles swapped for reusable and refillable bottles
- Single-use plastic plates and cutlery swapped for reusable ceramic plates and cutlery, or bamboo cutlery
- Cotton buds with plastic sticks swapped for cotton buds with paper or bamboo sticks
- Throw-away cups swapped for reusable cups or mugs for hot chocolate and milkshakes
- Plastic straws swapped for paper, metal or bamboo straws
- Single-use plastic bags swapped for reusable cloth or mesh bags
- Single-use plastic wrap swapped for waxed lunch wrap or a reusable lunchbox
- Single-use small chip and biscuit packets swapped for bigger packs emptied into reusable containers.
- Plastic-wrapped foods swapped for unwrapped food snacks (nude food)
- New plastic items swapped for products containing recycled plastic
- Plastic items swapped for bamboo, metal, cloth, cardboard, paper or beeswax wraps.

Plastic switch-a-roo

Can you see how you could make two to four changes in your home to help our oceans? What could you switch? How will you switch?

Be a part of the plastic solution

It's time to get active, support a program and be a change-maker. People are changing the world one plastic item at a time. They are working to create awareness and programs that help reduce the amount of plastic in the world. There are some fantastic programs out there. Some directly tackle the problem of plastics, while others encourage people to rethink the way they use plastic in daily life.

Plastic-free July

Join the global movement of going plastic free for July. Encourage your friends and family to join the 250 million people in 177 countries around the world who go plastic free for a whole month. Let's stand up and challenge ourselves to look after our planet and live more sustainably. Let's reduce our plastic footprint and make it as small as possible.

During July look for things made from aluminium, tin or other metals, glass, paper, cardboard, cotton, wool, linen, bamboo, timber or nude (no wrapping at all). Switch plastic items for other items, buy recycled goods, think about the plastic within the product or the plastic in the garment, and refuse single-use plastic items. Who knows, you might just start a plastic-free trend of your own?

Go strawkling

What is strawkling? It's snorkelling for straws. Strawkling is a great way to help the ocean and remove plastic straws from our beaches and seas. Volunteer snorkellers hunted for straws in Sydney Harbour and picked up more than 2500 straws from the sea floor. Australia uses 2.9 billion straws every year. We love our straws, and we don't always put them where they belong. Snorkelling is a great way to get out and be active in our oceans. Removing straws from the natural environment is very important. It prevents the plastic straw turning into tiny plastic confetti pieces and continuing to pollute the ocean and enter the food chain.

A plastic pelican made from ocean plastics washed onto the beach in Warrnambool, Victoria. The nurdles and plastic artwork reminds us of the impact we have on our ocean wildlife. A real pelican can collect up to 20 litres of seawater in one gulp when feeding – imagine all the plastics they could also pick up in their giant beaks!

COLLEEN HUGHSON

There are alternatives out there: straws made of paper, bamboo or metal all help reduce single-use plastic straws. Programs like StrawNoMore and The Last Straw have inspired businesses to stop giving away straws. We can refuse single-use straws or take our own when we are out and about, or just drink from a glass.

Get down and join a beach clean-up

Everyone loves a day at the beach, whether you live right near a beach, or if you are on holiday. Remember to Take 3 For the Sea. Take three pieces of rubbish home every time you go down to the beach. Take more than three if you can. Every bit of plastic counts, and when it's so close to the ocean, it is even more critical. One quick change in the wind and it could be out to sea, another item added to the plastic soup. You could change that. Pick up the plastic and put it in the bin where it won't blow away.

Perhaps you want to get involved in beach clean-ups. These are fantastic events which bring people together. Become part of **citizen-science** programs. Ocean clean-ups tell different stories about the rubbish that is collected. By recording the information from the items collected, the data can help us find solutions and help remove plastic waste before it gets into the oceans.

You never know what you might find. You might be lucky and find a message in a bottle sent years ago. You might find a plastic bottle or a plastic lid that's floated in from far away. Put your beach detective skills to the test, uncover an ocean mystery and help oceans at the same time.

Plan for an eco-celebration

Balloon-free events are an exciting way to express your ocean connection. Ocean-friendly parties inspired by Zoos Victoria are a great way to avoid plastics. By blowing bubbles, not balloons, you're thinking about the health of the oceans.

Celebrations can often be single-use plastic nightmares. But there are different ways to celebrate without letting the plastic get out of hand or a single balloon get out of sight.

Choose foods that are natural and fresh. Avoid food wrapped in plastic at the supermarket. If you are choosing chips, choose big packs. Big packs use less plastic than small individual packs. Remember to set up a soft plastics recycling bin and separate your waste for recycling. By separating soft plastic waste, it can have a new life – perhaps it will be remoulded into a plastic seat! If you take your soft plastics to a recycle drop-off point, it can be made into new outdoor furniture. It's much better than ending up in the ocean. Choose real plates or paper plates instead of plastic plates and serve drinks in glasses or bottles with paper straws. It may take a little bit of time to wash up, but the planet will thank you for it.

▲ Hooded plover under cover. Keeping ocean plastics from our beaches helps all types of ocean creatures. This hooded plover has been made of beach-washed ocean plastics including nurdles, inspiring us to think about the plastic we use each and every day. What could be avoided? What could be used instead?

Be a champion of change

Look around at the possibilities of where plastic could be replaced by a natural material. Here is a great idea to get you thinking: What about changing the plastic stick of lolly pops. Why aren't they available with bamboo sticks?

It is time to get active, rethink, reimagine and redesign a new plastic-free future! With a little bit of creativity, you could start a whole new movement. You and your friends could be the next inspirational ocean change-makers!

Chapter 10: Action for the oceans 111

DESIGN THINKING

Ideas for plastic-free futures

Design thinking is all about coming up with a new innovative solution to a real-world problem. It might be a way to stop plastics entering the ocean, replacing a plastic product or sharing a message!

Use these design thinking steps to bring your bright ideas to life:

The Brainstorm: Go solo or gather your friends around and brainstorm your 'plastic switching' ideas. No idea is too silly or crazy. Include them all!

▼

The Vote: Choose one idea that you want to bring to life.

▼

The Plan: Get started, drawing, sketching, researching and imagine the idea in action.

▼

The Share: Talk about the idea to see what people think! Listen to their suggestions, could they help improve the design or suggest a way to grow your new idea.

▼

The Rethink: Is there something that is missing? Is there a way to improve the idea? Redesign, rework and rethink. Keep testing ideas and reinventing! It may take many attempts to get the idea working but keep going!

▼

The Reach: Reach out and share your ideas! Whether it's fantastic or a flop it is definitely worth a try! Don't give up, try and try again! It will be worth it in the end because our oceans need you! Be a champion of your idea.

Be an ocean change-maker

The plastic ocean tide can be turned, and it can be changed. It's up to us to make the change. Start by saying 'no thanks' to plastic, make the switch to plastic-free products and be positive advocates for change. We have the knowledge and the ideas to innovate. We need to make changes now or our planet's oceans will continue to drown in plastic.

What will you do to help our oceans? The change starts with each one of us, making great choices with plastic alternatives, talking to people, having our voices heard, working with scientists, changing our behaviour and being proud to stand up for our oceans and being true ocean guardians. How will you make a difference?

Nurdle circle – beauty in the making. Nurdles removed off a beach can be made into inspiring artwork, encouraging us to think about our plastic oceans and what we can do to help.

COLLEEN HUGHSON

FURTHER INFORMATION

The following groups are all involved in ocean research and protection, and kindly provided information for this book. The author thanks them for their assistance:
- Better Buds: https://www.betterbuds.org.au/
- Fidra: https://www.fidra.org.uk/
- StrawNoMore: https://www.strawnomore.org/
- Take 3 for the Sea: https://www.take3.org/
- Tangaroa Blue Foundation: https://www.tangaroablue.org/
- Zoos Victoria fighting extinction website: When balloons fly seabirds die. https://www.zoo.org.au/balloons/

The following websites are all useful resources for you to learn more about ocean plastics:
- Australian Marine Conservation Society: https://www.marineconservation.org.au/ocean-plastic-pollution/
- National Geographic: https://www.nationalgeographic.com/environment/oceans/
- National Ocean and Atmospheric Administration (NOAA): https://www.noaa.gov/oceans-coasts
- Plastic Oceans: https://www.plasticoceans.org.au/
- Smithsonian: https://ocean.si.edu/ocean-life
- World Wildlife Fund (WWF): https://www.wwf.org.au/get-involved/plastics

GLOSSARY

Abyssal plain: the area of the ocean that is the deepest part of the sea floor.

Algae: these ancient, primitive plant-like organisms live in water but are neither plants nor animals. Like plants they make their own food by photosynthesis using energy from the sun. Unlike plants, algae have no roots, leaves or stems. They use water to keep themselves afloat to reach sunlight. Seaweeds are algae, but algae also grow in freshwater.

Algae bloom: a sudden increase in algae when the right environmental conditions occur.

Anticlockwise: the opposite way hands on a clock move to show time. Anticlockwise creates a left circular motion.

Atmosphere: layers of gases surrounding the Earth and keeping it warm. The main gas is nitrogen, then oxygen, argon, water vapour and carbon dioxide.

Bacteria: small single-celled organisms. They are found in or on all living things and almost all ecosystems in the world. Bacteria are essential to life.

Bamboo: a fast-growing plant that is part of the grass family. It makes strong fibres and wooden stems. Bamboo can be shredded to make a pulp and reformed into items, like knives, forks, spoons or plates. It is a great natural choice when switching from plastic products.

Bioaccumulation: the build-up or concentration of substances such as poisons in the body of living things, becoming more concentrated further up the food chain; plastic pollution is a source of poisons that accumulate in marine creatures.

Biofilm: a thin layer of microbes on objects. A biofilm forms on plastic items when they enter the ocean. The plastisphere is a biofilm.

Bioplastic: a plastic made from natural materials that can break down within a few months.

Blue carbon: the carbon dioxide captured by the world's oceans and coastal ecosystems. Plants (seagrasses and mangroves), phytoplankton and algae remove carbon dioxide from the atmosphere and store it in their cells using photosynthesis.

Broadcast spawning: when eggs and sperm are released on ocean currents to mix and become fertilised. Many creatures including fish, sea snails, sea stars and coral use broadcast spawning to reproduce.

Calcium: a mineral used by living things to make strong skeletons, bones, teeth and shells.

Carbon: an element that is found in diamonds, coal, petrol, the gas carbon dioxide, as well as plant and animal bodies. The way the carbon atoms are arranged differs in these forms of carbon. Carbon moves around the planet in the **carbon cycle**. Carbon makes up about 18 per cent of all living things.

Carbon cycle: the ways carbon is passed between the atmosphere, water, the Earth, and living things where it is used, transformed, stored and released, and changing from a gas to a solid at times.

Carbon dioxide: is made of two oxygen atoms and one carbon atom. It is found in the Earth's atmosphere as a gas. Carbon dioxide traps heat and creates a stable temperature on Earth. Too much carbon dioxide in the atmosphere makes the Earth's temperature rise.

Carbon sink: a place where carbon is held or stored. Living things in the ocean take in and store over 25 per cent of the world's carbon. As they die, they drift down and create a carbon sink on the ocean floor.

Chitin (ky-tin): a protein that makes hard, strong, water-resistant exoskeletons in insects and crustaceans such as lobsters, in the cell walls of fungi, the teeth-like structures in molluscs and the beaks of octopus and squid.

Chloroplasts (klor-o-plasts): a tiny part of the cells of plants and algae that contains chlorophyll, which absorbs sunlight to help the plant photosynthesise. Chloroplasts are green (chloro- means green in Greek).

Citizen science: people and the community involved in scientific research or data collection for such things as conservation programs, mapping species, etc.

Clockwise: a circular motion in the direction in which the hands on a clock move.

Cloth: a material woven from natural cotton, wool or other fibres to make fabric. Cloth fabric is used to make wearable clothes (jumpers, jeans) or can be used to clean up spills (dish cloth).

Coast: where the ocean or sea meets the land; continents are surrounded by coastlines.

Coccolithophores: single-celled marine algae that form plates or coccoliths from calcium; they occur in such numbers that they can cloud the water and produce

Glossary

more than 1.5 million tonnes of calcite a year, the mineral that forms marble, limestone and chalk; coccoliths are significant microfossils.

Colonise: find a place to live and grow; microbes colonise plastic pieces in the plastisphere.

Condense: when water vapour or gas cools it turns back into liquid (condensation). In the water cycle, clouds are an example of condensation. In the bathroom, steam from your hot shower condenses on the mirror.

Continents: very large land masses surrounded by oceans or seas. There are seven continents on Earth – Africa, Asia, Australia, Europe, North America, South America and Antarctica.

Continuous Plankton Recorder (CPR): a device pulled behind boats that is used to record plankton in the ocean.

Convection currents: are the circular movements of water or air that are different temperatures. Cool air or water sinks and warm air or water rises.

Coriolis Effect: the pattern of deflection taken by objects not firmly connected to the ground as they travel long distances around the Earth. In oceans, the Earth's rotation creates a water current that moves at a 45° angle. The wind above the water pushes the surface layers in the opposite direction, in a downward spiral.

CSIRO: Commonwealth Scientific and Industrial Research Organisation.

Currents: moving water; currents can be big or small, and are produced by winds, the rotation of the planet, and the temperature and density (heaviness) of water.

Cyanobacteria: bacteria that live in water and can photosynthesise; they were once incorrectly called blue-green algae.

Database: information stored and organised on a computer; data may be evidence or information used in scientific experiments.

Decompose: when things naturally break down into smaller pieces. It is the first stage in the recycling of nutrients that have been used by living things.

Decomposers: organisms that break down natural products back to their original form.

Diatoms: tiny single-celled algae that live in water and can photosynthesise. Diatoms have a cell wall made of calcium in the form of two overlapping shells, often with beautiful and elaborate patterns on them. Diatoms are a common form of phytoplankton.

Digestion, Digesting: breaking down food so the body can absorb the nutrients and expel the waste.

Digestive system: the system in the body that breaks down food, absorbs nutrients and expels waste.

Drop-off zones: the areas where the ocean floor drops down to the abyssal plain. They are found at the edge of a continental plate.

Ecosystem: a community of living things that interact with each other and their environment, for example, a coral reef or a pond. In a marine ecosystem, some of the living things are algae, phytoplankton, fish, mammals, sharks, jellyfish and reptiles, and the non-living things are water, sand, mud and rocks. All of these things interact and connect in the ecosystem.

Ekman Spiral: is a part of the Coriolis Effect. The Ekman Spiral describes the way water turns below the surface of the ocean. It is named after the Swedish oceanographer who described it, Vagn Ekman.

Element: a substance made from a single type of atom, such as iron, carbon, gold or oxygen. Elements are the building blocks of everything on Earth. They can be in the form of a gas, a liquid or a solid. Scientists know of 118 elements, but only 94 exist naturally on Earth.

Endemic: a living thing that is found naturally in one location or region.

Entangle: to become tangled in fishing equipment such as ropes, nets and fishing lines. Sea creatures and birds can starve, or be injured, drowned or killed when they become entangled.

Equator: an imaginary line that divides the Earth into the Northern Hemisphere and Southern Hemisphere.

Evaporate: to change from a liquid to a gas. Water evaporates in the water cycle: the sun heats the water, turning the water molecules into water vapour, an invisible gas.

Evolve: to gradually change, develop or improve. Living things change and adapt over long periods of time as a response to their natural environment or habitat. For example, an animal might develop changes in colour, pattern, body size or shape.

Exoskeleton: the outer skeleton of a living thing (exo = outside, skeleton = body frame or structure). Exoskeletons are a hard casing that supports and protects invertebrates (animals without backbones). Many creatures have exoskeletons including insects, crabs and seahorses.

Food chain: the feeding order of living things. Food chains connect living things to each other based on what they eat.

Food web: the feeding relationship between creatures. Food chains connect together to create food webs in habitats or ecosystems.

Fossil fuels: fuels made from life forms that lived on Earth millions of years ago. When they died their bodies decomposed and became fossilised over time, leaving elements like carbon and hydrogen behind. The three most important fossil fuels are oil, gas and coal. Oil can be used to make products like plastics.

Fragment: a small piece of something that was once a whole. Plastics break up into smaller pieces which can be called fragments.

Friction: when one object moves against another, friction is the force that resists the movement. When any two things rub together, they cause friction – rough surfaces cause more friction, smooth surfaces cause less.

Fungi: a simple living thing that is not a plant or animal, and can break down organic material. It grows in the dark, making its own energy.

Geochemical scientist: a person who studies the chemistry of the Earth, including the chemical processes that occur when rocks and minerals are formed.

Geographical barrier: something that physically prevents the spreading of organisms. This could be because of temperature (climate), land or water bodies. The open ocean acts as a physical barrier for larvae due to its size and depth; larvae can cross the barrier by floating with assistance from objects, such as pumice.

Global Positioning System (GPS): a navigation system that uses satellites orbiting the Earth to identify a location.

Great Pacific Garbage Patch: an area of the Pacific Ocean were ocean plastics collect. The northern ocean gyre brings in plastics from around the world. There are two garbage patches, the biggest is between Hawaii and California, and the second is near Japan. There are also garbage patches in gyres in all the other oceans.

Greenhouse gas: any gas that traps heat in Earth's atmosphere. These gases let sunlight pass through to the Earth but stop heat escaping into space. The natural greenhouse gases are water vapour, carbon dioxide, nitrous oxide, ozone and methane. Chlorofluorocarbons are artificial greenhouse gases that also damage the ozone layer.

Gyres: slow-moving, ocean-wide, swirling currents that flow anticlockwise in the Southern Hemisphere and clockwise in the Northern Hemisphere. Gyres are powered by the wind, the land around them and the Earth's rotation. There are five ocean gyres, which occur in the Indian, North Atlantic, South Atlantic, North Pacific and South Pacific oceans. In the centre of gyres are calm waters where ocean debris accumulates.

Habitat: a place where organisms naturally live that has what they need to survive and grow, such as water, food, shelter, mates and a suitable climate or temperature.

Hemisphere: half of a sphere such as the Earth or a planet. Earth has two hemispheres, a Northern and a Southern hemisphere. When it is summer in one hemisphere, it is winter in the other.

Invertebrate: a living thing that does not have a backbone or internal skeleton. Invertebrates have an exoskeleton to protect their bodies.

Krill: a small shrimp-like crustacean that is an important food source for whales.

Larvae: the young of animals without backbones. The larvae of marine species may drift in the ocean until they change into their adult form and settle in a suitable habitat where they can live.

Lava: a hot liquid rock that comes out from the Earth's core onto the surface, creating volcanos and ocean seafloor vents. When lava cools it hardens to form rocks.

Magma: the hot liquid rock continually moving inside the Earth's core. Magma can reach temperatures of over 1200°C.

Magnetic field: the area around a magnet where there is a magnetic force. A magnetic field creates a positive or negative force. The Earth has a magnetic field, created by the movement of magma in the Earth's core. It is an invisible force that can be observed when using a compass. Migratory species use the Earth's magnetic field when travelling long distances.

Marine debris: floating objects in the ocean; ocean plastics form a large part of marine debris.

Metal: natural elements used to make strong, long-lasting products. Metal can hold heat and transfer electricity. There are many different types of metals including steel, tin, aluminium and silver.

Microbes: minute, simple living things such as bacteria, viruses, algae and fungi. They can be found everywhere, in water, air, soil, and inside and outside our bodies. Some are helpful, and some are harmful.

Microfibres: extremely fine plastic fibres from fabric such as polyester or fleece.

Microplastics: small pieces of plastic less than 5 millimetres in size. They are harmful to marine and aquatic life. Microplastics can be formed by larger plastics breaking up into smaller pieces. They can also be purposely made into items like nurdles or even microbeads for beauty products.

Microscopic: so small that it can only be seen through a microscope.

Middens: a mound of discarded shells and food scraps indicating a site where Indigenous people lived.

Migrate: when a living thing moves from one place to another for food, shelter or mates.

Migration: journeys over small or large distances, as the season's change or daily, but usually refers to long seasonal journeys.

Molecule: two or more atoms bonded together tightly to form substances that can be solid, liquid or a gas. The form of the substance depends on the atoms and the way they are arranged. For example, two hydrogen atoms and one oxygen atom make water (H_2O).

Nanoplastics: extremely small particles of plastic (1 billion nanoparticles can fit on the head of a pin) that can cross cell walls and cause unknown damage to living things, including people.

Natural: made by or in nature, not artificial.

Nitrogen: a gas found in the Earth's atmosphere. Nitrogen is important for all living things as it helps them grow.

Nostril: two small openings that are connected to a creature's airway for breathing. Nostrils can be permanently open (like on a bird's beak) or they can open and close (like in mammals such as a seal).

Nurdles: small hard plastic pellets the size of a grain of rice and shaped like a lentil.

Nutrients: the parts of food that feed living things, providing them with energy to live and grow.

Oceanographer: a scientist who studies the biological and physical aspects of the ocean.

Olfactory nose: an area or nose (nostril) capable of smelling or receiving chemical signals that food or predators are close. Fish have nostrils and pits that can detect smell underwater, while seabirds have nostrils on their beak that can receive smells over long distances.

Organic: anything relating to living things; natural things or materials that are made in nature that can break down.

Organism: any living thing – it can be a plant, animal, bacteria or fungi. The same kind of organisms are called a species. Organisms have basic needs to survive, including water, food, shelter and, in some species, reproductive mates.

Oxygen: a chemical element. It is a colourless, odourless, tasteless gas that is necessary for some life forms on Earth.

Pelagic: a species living in open ocean waters.

Persistent Organic Pollutants (POPs): industrially manufactured chemicals that stay in the environment for a very long time and harm living things, for example pesticides, drugs and plastics.

Photodegradation: when materials, such as plastic, change because of light. Light can cause the plastic to become harder and more brittle, resulting in cracks appearing or the colour fading.

Photosynthesis (foto-syn-the-sis): the process by which green plants and algae use energy from sunlight to make their own food from water and carbon dioxide, and giving off oxygen.

Phytoplankton (fy-toe-plank-ton): microscopic plants, algae, bacteria and other plant-like organisms that live in water. Like land plants, phytoplankton can photosynthesise.

Plankton: tiny drifting plants and plant-like organisms (phytoplankton) or animals (zooplankton) that live in the surface layers of water. Some zooplankton, like jellyfish, can be quite large, other zooplankton are microscopic or tiny and includes the eggs and larvae of fish and other living things.

Plastic: a lightweight material that is made by people using petroleum (crude oil) and chemicals. Plastic is used in many different products, for example straws, containers, cups, phones and cutlery.

Plastic footprint: the measure of the amount of plastic that someone creates each day, month or year.

Plastisphere: life such as microscopic bacteria and algae growing on the surface of ocean plastic.

Pollution: something that when added to the environment is harmful to living things.

Polymer: made of single molecules called monomers, joined together to make chains called polymers.

Predators: creatures that feed on other living things to gain a food source or energy. A predator can hunt or capture prey to eat it.

Prototype: the first design of a new invention or product that is tested to check for problems and to prompt new ideas.

Pumice: formed when lava bubbles up to the surface of the ocean. As the lava cools it releases gas bubbles, making the rock light and aerated. Pumice floats on the ocean's surface. When large underwater volcanoes or vents release lava, the pumice can form large floating masses, sometimes called pumice rafts.

Purse seine net: a net designed to catch a whole school of fish; these nets are large and cause serious problems when they are lost at sea.

Recycle: collect used products and materials to process and to make new products or materials.

Research: investigate carefully to find out information, facts or principles; scientists conduct research to find out answers to questions.

Rotation: turning on an axis; the Earth rotates once every 24 hours, and this rotation produces day and night.

Salinity: a measure of the salt that is dissolved in water; the saltiness of seawater can be lower when it is near rivers or near the equator, and higher under sea ice in the Arctic or Antarctica. Ocean water has a salt concentration of about 3.5 per cent.

Salps: transparent, barrel-shaped marine animals that live in groups. They are filter feeders and float in the ocean.

Sample: a scientific collection of items to investigate, for example organisms, soil, air or water.

Sedentary: living things that live their lives attached to a surface or only move small distances.

Sediment: sand, silt, mud or other materials that cover the bottom surface of oceans, lakes, rivers or streams. Sediment also contains pieces of dead organic matter (plants and animals), and stores carbon in sediment layers.

Senses: marine animals have senses: they can taste, smell and see. Some marine creatures have the ability to detect electrical or magnetic fields, to echolocate, and to see infrared and ultraviolet light.

Single-use: something that can only be used once such as cups, bags and wrappers.

Species: a group of living things that have the same common characteristics like physical appearance or biology and can produce fertile living offspring.

Subpolar: on Earth, the zone found close to the North and South poles but not within the Arctic or Antarctic circles.

Subtropical: on Earth, the zone found between the tropics (near the equator) and temperate zones (between the subtropics and the subpolar zones).

Synchronised: events that happen at the same time. In the ocean, the events can depend on environmental conditions like weather, tides and temperature. Coral spawning is a synchronised event.

Technofossil: a word used by scientists to describe waste left from plastic products that will be found in future fossil records.

Tectonic plates: continents sit on plates of the Earth's crust that are larger than the continents and also form the sea floor. Tectonic plates float over the Earth's inner mantle. Under the ocean, the continental plates are thinner. The continental plates drop off into deep trenches under the ocean.

Theory: an idea or thought that is tested to work out if it is possible. Scientists conduct experiments to test theories.

Toxins: poisonous substances that cause harm and can build up over time to unsafe levels.

Tropical: on Earth, the zone found on either side of the equator.

Upwelling current: a current of cold water rich in nutrients that rises to the surface near coastlines.

Vapour: gas, such as water vapour.

Virus: a type of germ that often causes sicknesses such as influenza and colds; viruses are too small to be seen by ordinary microscopes and can only survive and multiply inside the cells of a host (the organisms they infect).

Waste: any substance that is discarded or thrown away after use. Waste can be made or manufactured. Plastic becomes waste when it is thrown away. Waste can also be natural, made from natural functions of living things, including carbon dioxide (breathing) and poo (digestion).

Water cycle: the movement of water between oceans, rivers and lakes into the atmosphere as water vapour and back to Earth as rain, snow, hail or sleet.

Weathering: a natural process that slowly breaks apart a material like stone or plastic. Heat, wind, water, living things and other natural forces can cause weathering.

Zooplankton: tiny animals or animal-like organisms that float or swim in water; zooplankton and phytoplankton are the basis of the food web in marine and freshwater environments.

INDEX

A
abyssal plain 18
algae 13, 14, 27
anchovies 58
atmosphere 9, 12, 15

B
bacteria 14, 45, 58
bamboo 101
beach clean-up 109
beach detectives 83
bioaccumulation 69
biofilm 45, 58
bioplastics 80, 82
blue carbon 15
broadcast spawning 35

C
carbon 15
carbon dioxide 9, 15
carbon sink 15
citizen scientist 83–84, 109
climate 15, 17
continent 18
continental shelf 19
Continuous Plankton
    Recorder 71
Coriolis Effect 24
currents 26–28, 32
    Antarctic
        Circumpolar 27
    boundary 29
    break-away eddies 30
    convection 26
    East Australian 28
    Indonesian Through
        Flow 28
    Leeuwin 27, 28
    upwelling 26

D
decompose 45, 51
design thinking 111
diatoms 13, 14
digestion 51, 62
dolphinfish 95
drop-off zones 21

E
eco-celebration 109
ecosystem 10
equator 9, 30

F
fish eggs 57, 66–67
food chain 62, 69
food webs 26, 60–61, 62
fossil fuels 49–50
fulmar 77
fungi 51, 80

G
geochemical scientists 35
ghost nets 74
Global Positioning
    System 33
Great Pacific Garbage
    Patch 29, 39–40, 46
    plastic pieces 40
    size 40–41
greenhouse gas 15, 17
gyres 21–24, 26, 28–29
    subpolar 30
    subtropical 30
    tropical 30

H
habitat 9–10
hemisphere 22
hermit crab 104
hooded plovers 66–67, 110

I
ice cap 16
Indigenous rangers 75
invertebrate 45

J
jellyfish 32, 57, 63

K
krill 58, 61

L
larvae 35
lava 34
limpets 36
litter traps 96
lobsters 81

M
magnetic field 33
Mariana Trench 18
marine debris 83
marine entanglement 73
microbes 51
    land 51
    marine 44, 45, 51
microfibre 46
microplastic 46, 55
microscopic 13, 44
    phytoplankton 13
    plankton 13–14, 47
midden 54
migration 28
mimicry 57
molecule 12

N
nanoplastic 46–47
North Pole 9
nurdles 52, 57, 66–67, 89
nutrients 10, 26, 27, 30

O
oceanographer 28
oceans 8–10
    Arctic 9
    Atlantic 9
    Indian 9
    Pacific 9
    Southern 9, 27
olfactory 57

opportunistic feeders 63
organism 10
oxygen 9, 15

P

Persistent Organic
  Pollutants 68–69
photosynthesis 13, 14
phytoplankton 13–14
plankton 13, 49
plastic
  bags 30, 57, 97, 103
  bottles 39, 47, 52
  floating rubbish 38–41
  footprint 100
  free 107
  pieces 39, 40, 43
  single-use 42, 106
  switching ideas
    105–106
  weathering 43–44
plastisphere 45, 47
polar ice caps 9

pollutants 68–69
pollution 23, 80
predators 45
pumice raft 35

R

recycle 49, 52–53, 88
research 40
reuse 101
rotation 24–25

S

salps 57
samples 55
sand hoppers 66–67
sea anemones 63
sealions 89
seas
  Arafura 10
  Black 10
  Caribbean 10
  Mediterranean 10
  Red 10

sediment 15, 49
short-tailed
  shearwaters 65, 76
silkworms 81
South Pole 9
strawkling 107
straws 88, 93

T

technofossils 55
tectonic plate 18
temperature
  air 23
  Earth's 9, 16, 17
  water 26–28
turtles
  green 63–64
  leatherback 32

V

viruses 14
volcanic eruption 34

W

water cycle 12
  condense 12
  evaporate 12
  vapour 12
whales
  humpback 28
  southern right 73
wind 23
  friction 23
wandering albatross 7

Z

zooplankton 10, 13

www.ingramcontent.com/pod-product-compliance
Lightning Source LLC
Chambersburg PA
CBHW041352070426

42633CB00013B/16